BALLER B⚽YS

-VS-

THE BULLDOZERS

Venessa Taylor

illustrated by Kenneth Ghann

Aim for your goals !

~~Hashtag~~ PRESS

Published in Great Britain by Hashtag Press 2023

A CIP catalogue for this book is available from the British Library.

Paperback ISBN 9781913835194

Typeset in Calibri 12.25/16 by Hewer Typesetting
Printed in Great Britain by Clays Ltd, Elcograf S.p.A.

Hashtag PRESS

HASHTAG PRESS BOOKS
Hashtag Press Ltd
Kent, England, United Kingdom
Email: info@hashtagpress.co.uk
Website: www.hashtagpress.co.uk
Twitter: @hashtag_press

For my Grandson Rayne, every time I watch you play football, I feel inspired to write. Thank you for being my wingman and sharing your ideas with me and checking that my writing is authentic.

In loving memory of Reece Darcheville

For my brother Raymond, anytime I watch you
play basketball I am inspired to write. Thank you for
being my whole world and for sharing your passion with
me and teaching me that my voice will be heard.

In loving memory of Rocco O'Donnell.

CHAPTER 1

Not Enough Football!

"Tandeep, pass!" Shay yelled.

Tandeep crossed the ball down the centre, away from the Stokey Town midfielders towards Shay. Running down the centre of the pitch, chasing the ball, the two Stokey Town midfielders were hot on Shay's heels. But Shay's lack of fitness was clear to see, when both Stokey Town midfielders sped past him, taking the ball with them.

Shay stopped, breathing hard. He threw his arms up in the air in frustration. He could feel the tears welling up in his eyes, but he didn't want to cry in front of everyone, so he took several long, deep breaths until the feeling passed.

Stokey Town manoeuvred the ball back into the direction of AC United's goal, out running AC's defenders Blessing and Troy. Stokey Town left AC chasing the ball, leaving their opponents unmarked. This enabled Stokey Town to find their unmarked striker and pass him the ball, which he neatly and precisely tucked into the back of the AC net.

The Stokey Town fans cheered, whistled and clapped, encouraging their players on, while AC looked on in shock wondering what had just happened.

"You lot, mark up!" Maxwell, the AC goalie yelled at the team. He was disappointed in himself for letting the goal in, and he felt frustrated with the team for not stopping the Stokey Town striker from getting through to score. Immediately, AC ran closer to the opponents they should have been marking. Shay made sure that this time he was marking his opponent close enough to touch his arm.

"Come on boys, keep your heads up!" Coach Joe yelled from the side-lines.

It was 1-0 to Stokey Town with five minutes left of play and they were running rings around AC. Frankie finally managed to get possession of the ball and tackled a Stokey Town midfielder. Frankie fought hard to keep the ball but was eventually forced to cross it to his teammate (and least favourite person) Hassan once he realised that he couldn't outskill his opponent.

"Take a shot Hassan! Take a shot!" Coach Joe screamed as Hassan hurtled towards the Stokey Town goal.

A Stokey Town defender went in for a tackle, kicking Hassan's ankle. Hassan fell to the floor rolling in agony.

The referee blew the whistle and shouted, "Penalty," and he pointed at AC United.

AC clapped their hands in agreement with the ref's decision and looked over at Coach Joe for the next move.

Yes, a chance for us to win one back, Shay thought.

"Shay, you take it and the rest of you move forward ready for a rebound!" Coach Joe ordered from the side-line.

Hassan stood up on one leg and rolled his ankle. He looked over at Shay and gave him a thumbs-up.

Running into position, Shay steadied himself to take the shot. He was usually good at taking penalties, so he wasn't sure why his legs were shaking, and his heart was beating so fast. Maybe it was the pressure of knowing that it could be their only chance to get a goal and equalise.

"Come on Shay, you've got this!"

He knew his mum's voice anywhere. She was always the loudest of all the parents.

With all the screaming and yelling going on around him, Shay had to block out the noise and focus. He took a deep breath to steady his nerves and visualised where he was going to place the ball. He wanted it to land in the top right-hand corner of the net. The goal-keeper looked tall for an under-ten and was hopping about from foot to foot, his arms stretched out wide.

Shay ran up to the football, pulled back his right leg and kicked it with such force that it fired into the top right-hand corner of the net just like he'd planned! Shay had never heard the AC fans cheer so loud. The final whistle blew, and the game ended on a draw.

Coach Joe waved them over. His slim, six-foot-six frame towered over the tired players as they flopped down on the ground. "It was your first friendly of the season and we could see you were giving it your all, so well done. However, it seems like most of your football over the summer must have been online and not in the park!" Coach Joe raised an eyebrow.

Shay and Frankie looked at each other sheepishly knowing that they had spent most of the summer playing FIFA.

"Think of today as a warm-up for when the season starts in a couple of weeks," Coach Joe continued.

Coach Kaan nodded in agreement. His cap was pulled down covering his low cropped hair. Shay noticed Coach Kaan was wearing a necklace with a blue eye symbol.

"Coach Kaan, what's that eye?" Shay asked pointing at the necklace.

Coach Kaan held it. "Oh, it's called a Nazar. Lost of Turkish people wear them or have them in their homes. As part of our culture, we believe it keeps us safe and brings us good luck . . . and talking of luck, I think you know that we were lucky to get a draw today. Thankfully, we've got time to improve, and we don't have a full squad yet, as Troy and Jamie are still away. We're also expecting a new player to join us soon, so we will get better as a team."

"What new player?" Shay asked.

"You'll find out on Friday," Coach Kaan replied, and Shay huffed. He hated not knowing what was going on.

"Maybe we should all wear a Nazar necklace for luck," Oscar joked.

"My dad's Irish and he has a four-leaf clover for luck," Frankie said.

Coach Joe scoffed. "Guys, luck? Really!

"You gotta work hard, can't just rely on luck.
If you don't stay active, you're gonna get
stuck!
You can't sit still and rely on luck.
Take time to practice, you'll see it's worth it.
You know the old saying . . .
Practice makes perfect!"

If Coach Joe hadn't got into football, he would have definitely been a rapper. AC clapped their hands and Coach Joe gave a mock bow.

"Now I need everyone on time and ready to work hard to start our pre-season training," Coach Joe said, serious again. "Let's get our fitness even better than last season. Everyone up!" The players stood, dusting off the grass from their shorts. "Before you go off and enjoy the rest of your day, right hand in."

Everyone huddled together and put their right hands into the middle on top of each other.

Coach Joe shouted, "3, 2, 1!"

And they shouted back, "UNITED!"

CHAPTER 2

Changes

It was Thursday night and Frankie couldn't sleep due to the unusually hot September weather. Although it was way past his bedtime, he was thirsty and needed some water. The bedroom door creaked as Frankie carefully opened it. Creeping down the stairs he was surprised to see the living room door open and his parents sitting down on the couch with their backs to him.

"It's a really nice house Colin, with a bigger garden and four nice-sized bedrooms. It would be great for the kids," his mum Tina said.

Frankie sat down on the bottom step confused. *What house?*

"The kitchen will need doing up, but we can make it our own and it has two bathrooms!" she continued.

Even though he knew he shouldn't be earwigging, Frankie was frozen to the spot. His head began to spin with a thousand thoughts.

When did they decide we were moving? They can't be serious. I've just made the team! How can they do this to me?

No longer thirsty, Frankie crept back to his room, careful not to alert anyone. He climbed into bed and stared up at the ceiling. With all the questions he now had, he couldn't get back to sleep.

*

The next morning Frankie sat at the breakfast table with his head in his hands. He was exhausted and keeping his head up required too much effort. His little sister Katie was on her best form today, singing and dancing around the kitchen, begging him to watch her. She kept poking him to get his attention.

"Katie, just leave me alone!" he finally snapped.

Katie's mouth dropped open before her bottom lip began to tremble, and she burst into loud, noisy sobs.

"Frankie, don't speak to your sister like that," Tina snapped. "What is the matter with you this morning? I was just going to tell you how good your summer project is and now this."

Frankie didn't answer, instead he turned his head away from his mum.

"Katie, come here love, don't cry. Frankie, apologise to your sister!" Tina hugged Katie and glared at Frankie over her shoulder.

"Sorry Katie." Frankie sighed as he pushed his cereal around in the bowl with his spoon.

"And can you stop messing around with your food," Tina said.

"I'm not hungry," Frankie mumbled back.

"Really? Okay fine, go get your trainers on then. We need to get the last bits of school uniform for you and your sister."

Whilst doing up his laces, Frankie wondered what was the point in getting more uniform if they were moving? He couldn't believe his parents were doing this and hadn't even spoken to him. He wanted to ask them about it but then that would make the whole moving thing real, and he didn't want it to be.

*

Meanwhile, a few doors down, Shay was stuck into his school summer project – endangered birds. All he wanted to do was go online and play with his friends, but his mum had put her foot down. No games until the school project was finally done.

Shay stared at his work feeling proud of himself. It was hard but he was finally finished on his summer project about nightingales.

"Mum, can you look at it for me please? My teacher said anyone who does a good conservation project and brings it in on the first day back will get ten house points straight away," Shay explained.

"Let me just finish putting your school uniform away and see if Rayne is still okay playing in the garden," Joanne said.

Fifteen minutes later Joanne went to sit with her eldest at the kitchen table.

"I coloured the nightingale in and wrote this as the title," Shay said pointing to the title at the top of the first page.

"Nightingales, the singing birds," Joanne read out. "I think that's the perfect title, well done Shay. So, why are they a protected bird?"

"Because their numbers are going down as they are losing their habitat. I also wrote this bit about their beautiful singing and that not many people get to hear it. Did you know that it's actually the male bird singing at night trying to attract a female?"

"Why don't people get to hear it?"

"Ermm, let me see what I wrote, oh yeah, because they're like owls, they usually come out at night."

"Oh, are they nocturnal?"

"Yeah, that's the word, thanks Mum, I'm gonna use it in my writing, it'll impress my teacher."

Joanne kissed him on the forehead. "Shay it's brilliant. See what happens when you focus!" She gently nudged him, and Shay laughed.

"I know, I know . . . can I play FIFA now?"

CHAPTER 3

May The Best Baller Win!

That evening, Shay was in his living room, playing an intense game of FIFA online with Frankie.

"I can't wait for the season to really get started. This season belongs to *us*; the dream team are back in business!" Shay said excitedly into his headphones. His fingers moved swiftly over the control buttons. "Frankie man, I'm so happy you made the main team this season. Last season, when you came on as a sub, you were so good. I knew this time you would make it through at the trials. You're so fast and you've got skills, but for your shots, *please* make sure you're wearing your glasses so you can see properly."

"Yeah, I will." Frankie chuckled. "I wear them most of the time now and always for football. I'm making sure that I can see my target!"

"I saw Troy at the barbers yesterday and he was getting his Afro shaped up. I got my sides faded and my mum twisted the top to look like Tyrone Mings'," Shay said. "The barbers was packed with kids getting their hair cut for school this week. That's how you can always tell when the summer holidays are over."

"I can't wait to see the whole team at training," Frankie said.

"Oh, yeah, even Hassan?" Shay teased.

"Well, of course not Hassan! Last season he was so rude to me just because I was in the development team. He was always trying to leave me out and didn't invite me to his dad's restaurant, remember?" Frankie frowned, still annoyed at the memory.

"Yeah, he was a bit much. I think he was jealous of you because you're faster than him. Anyway, don't worry about him, you've made the team now. And so far, he's been alright with you."

"True, and this time I'm coming to his restaurant if we're invited and I'm going to eat all the kebabs!" Frankie quipped and they burst out laughing.

"Do you know what? This season I'm going all out," Shay said. "I'm going for Baller Boy and I'm going to work so hard that Coach Reece will have no choice but to choose me. I even tried to get my dad to buy me the rainbow-coloured sock boots. I told him that they would help improve my performance, but he said they were too expensive and that I would just have to use my natural ability."

"Wait! I was thinking the same thing," Frankie said.

"What about my natural talent?" Shay joked.

"No, about me going for Baller Boy."

Shay frowned, surprised at Frankie's comment.

But he's only just made the team, he's a good player, but I think he has a lot of work to do, Shay thought to himself.

Not wanting to discourage his best friend or fall out with him like last season, Shay said out loud, "May the best footballer win!"

Frankie had worked so hard in the development squad and to *finally* get selected for the main team meant everything to him. He was determined to be crowned this season's Baller Boy.

What's the harm in a bit of friendly competition between friends? Frankie thought.

He had fallen out with Shay over football before and he didn't want that to happen again.

Frankie wanted to tell Shay that he had heard his parents talking about moving house. He needed to let this big secret out but then Shay yawned through the headphones.

Maybe this isn't the best time, Frankie thought.

From behind him, Frankie heard his front door open, and he knew it was his dad coming back from work. His dad was a firefighter and Frankie adored him.

Shay sighed loudly. "Frankie, I've got to go now. My mum says after six weeks off school I've got to get back into my *bedtime routine*," Shay said mimicking his mum's voice. "We don't even go back to school till next week!"

"I can't believe we're going into Year Five," Frankie said.

"Oh, she's coming! Frankie, I'd better go, I'll see you tomorrow . . . yes Mum, I'm logging off," and a second later Shay was gone.

Sitting in his bedroom, alone with his thoughts, Frankie wondered if he should speak to his dad about going for Baller Boy this season but then he remembered his parent's conversation.

What if Dad tells me not to bother because I'll be leaving AC soon?

The thought of leaving made Frankie feel like bursting into tears.

No, he decided. *I won't say anything for now.*

CHAPTER 4

Back Together

The first few weeks of the new football season were always exciting for everyone on the team. Chatting away excitedly, AC United greeted each other whilst also looking out for the new player Coach Kaan had told them about.

Jamie, who was affectionately known as the 'fidgety boy,' was back, and as usual was on the go. Last season the players had learnt that Jamie has ADHD. His mum Kathy was always nearby keeping a close eye on him.

While strolling across the grass, Shay stopped and observed Jamie, who was performing perfect cartwheels back-to-back. His red, shoulder-length hair was flying all over the place. A ball flew in Jamie's direction and Shay watched him stop his cartwheel, pass the ball back and then resume his cartwheel, all without pausing to take a breath!

Jamie's lips were moving, as if he was talking to someone. Shay thought it was safe to assume he was humming away to himself. Shay waved at him, but Jamie appeared not to notice. He was now too busy trying to balance on his hands! Nearby, Jamie's mum Kathy today with green hair (every few weeks she liked to dye her hair a different colour) spotted Shay waving so she waved back to him.

Everyone was crowded around Oscar who was unusually early. His blonde hair had been cut so short it looked like he had spikes on his head.

"So, on YouTube, I've got over 1,500 subscribers." Oscar puffed up his chest. "I'm planning to give Kevin Hart a run for his money. Trust me, any day now some big agent will see my videos, snap me up and I'll be all over your screens."

"Yeah right." Blessing rolled his eyes. He spotted Shay and fist bumped him. "That was my uncle's barber shop you were in the other day. He shaped you up good." Blessing admired Shay's fade and twists.

Most of the team were present but when Shay looked over at Frankie, he noticed the sour expression on his face. As he followed the direction Frankie was looking in, he saw why . . . Hassan.

Hassan was swaggering towards them with his shoulders back, chest out, and a wide grin plastered on his face. He was the tallest of all the players and the most competitive. On his feet he wore the high-top rainbow-sock boots that Shay wanted and across his shoulder he carried the matching rainbow-coloured sports bag.

Shay looked at Hassan's boots with envy and hoped his dad might let him have them for his birthday, but he knew it was unlikely as they were so expensive.

Hassan walked into the centre of the group and immediately started talking over everyone else. "My uncle queued up early outside the sports shop to get these for me and my cousin. We got two of the first pairs released." He balanced on his left foot, lifting his right foot up to show off the rainbow-sock boots, as the boys admired his new footwear.

"Nice boots, Hassan," Frankie commented but Hassan ignored him.

Frankie swallowed hard.

"Our favourite show-off's back. Let's all give him a round of applause!" Oscar said, clapping his hands and making the boys snigger.

Hassan's face went red and he walked off in a huff.

"Anyway, did any of you hear about the fields being sold?" Oscar asked.

"What fields?" Maxwell frowned.

"These fields!" Oscar said holding his arms out. "Marshals!"

"Whatever, funny guy," Blessing said, and they all laughed.

Oscar crossed his arms over his chest and scowled at them.

"Where did you hear that?" Shay asked.

"From my neighbour who works for the council," Oscar answered.

"You serious or is this another one of your jokes?" Frankie raised an eyebrow at him.

"Oh, get lost, you lot! You wait and see!" Oscar snapped before walking away.

"Oscar come back!" Shay called out after him. "We're not sure if you're joking or not."

"If you are, it's not funny!" Blessing yelled in Oscar's direction.

"Exactly! Imagine anyone trying to sell our pitch? I don't think so!" Shay said.

CHAPTER 5

No Girls Allowed

Shay spotted two people walking towards them wearing turbans, and knew it was Tandeep and his dad. Last season, Shay and Tandeep had developed a good scoring partnership. Tandeep would pass the ball to Shay in the centre of the pitch, then Tandeep would sprint forward past the opposing defender. Shay would then quickly play a neat through ball back to Tandeep. He would play the ball into the box where Shay would be waiting to tuck it into the net, leaving the opposition scratching their heads and wondering what had just happened. Coach Joe had worked them hard to get this play right and it always worked. The memories brought a smile to Shay's face.

"I wonder who made it through the trials?" Shay asked the rest of the team. "Apart from Frankie, I thought there were a couple of other talented players."

The trials had been three weeks ago, during the summer break, and all the AC players had been re-selected for the team.

"Can you believe those two girls that tried out for our team? What a joke!" Oscar said rolling his eyes and smirking.

"Yeah, as if they would be good enough to join AC!" Blessing added.

"That girl was good," Maxwell said.

"What girl?" Shay frowned as he tried to remember.

"Oh, I know which one you mean!" Frankie said. "She was wearing black and purple boots. The one whose shots went in every time and was *almost* as fast as me and Hassan."

"Oh her." Shay shrugged. "Yeah, she was alright!"

Shay was certain a girl couldn't be as good as him at shooting and scoring.

"I think her name was Ashleigh or something like that. Anyway, who cares if girls join us?" Maxwell said. "Some girls are really good players. Look at Sam Kerr and Georgia Stanway, and the Lionesses won the Euros!"

"But they're adults. Most girls our age aren't good at football," Blessing argued.

"That's not true. Alexia on Essex Road Giants is really good," Maxwell said.

"Well, there's no girls good enough for AC," Blessing insisted with a mouth full of crisps.

"I thought Ashleigh was alright," Frankie added.

"AC United is definitely an all-boys team. I agree with Blessing," Hassan said as he marched over. "There are no girls good enough to join us and there never will be!"

Shay would never admit it out loud, but he secretly agreed.

"Well, I don't agree, I think if they're good enough to join us then they should be allowed," Frankie insisted.

"I bet you're just looking for a girlfriend," Oscar teased, and the others laughed.

"Oh, whatever Oscar," Frankie replied. He could see a familiar face near the main gates and pointed. "Look!"

Everyone turned to look. With a fresh, low trimmed Afro, Troy was trotting over. Finally, the team were all here!

"Boys!" Coach Joe yelled, motioning with his large hands for the players to come closer to him as he walked towards them. He had been standing on the other side of the pitch, behind the goal, chatting away to an older Black man with shoulder length greying locs, dressed in a Hammers football top. He was holding the hand of a child dressed in an AC training kit.

Frankie grinned to himself as he recognised the child from the trials, grateful that his glasses were helping him to see better.

"Right guys, before we get started, I just need to remind you all about our no nuts or fish policy, we need to remember that Shay is allergic to them. I'll also send out a reminder in the WhatsApp group. Now, I'd like you to meet a player who came to our trials and who'll be joining our team." Coach Joe looked at the two people standing at the far end of the pitch beside the goal and used his hand to gesture for the child to come over.

"This is Ashleigh, and I'm expecting you all to make her feel welcome," Coach Joe said.

Ashleigh was wearing a brand-new AC United training kit, a well-used pair of purple and black football boots and a huge smile across her face, showing off perfect teeth and dimples. She wore her long Afro hair in one large bunch that sat loosely on the top of her head making her look taller than she was. In fact, she was about as tall as Shay.

"Welcome Ashleigh," Coach Joe said. "I made up a special rap for you.

"You're the first girl to try out for this team,
And at the trials you played like a dream.
You earned your place, so you got invited
So welcome Ashleigh to AC United!"

"Thanks Coach, that was great!" Ashleigh grinned.

Shay's eyes bulged and Hassan's mouth dropped open.

"Guys, introduce yourselves and tell Ashleigh your position. Let's start with you, Mr Comedian." Coach Joe pointed at Oscar.

"I'm Oscar, I play midfield and I'm here to entertain you!" Oscar said in an animated voice before he gave a mock bow. Everyone laughed.

Shay didn't understand why Oscar was so calm about it. He couldn't believe that Ashleigh was joining their team!

She better not be a striker, no way could she be my competition, he thought.

Ashleigh looked at Shay and for a split second he thought he had said that out loud. He quickly realised that she was waiting for him to introduce himself.

"I'm Shay and I'm a striker," Shay said.

Ashleigh smiled showing off her dimples, but Shay barely returned it.

"Hi, I'm Frankie! I play midfield and I remember you from the trials," Frankie said. "You were really good."

"Thank you," Ashleigh replied grinning.

After most of the players had introduced themselves, Coach Joe stood next to Jamie and Tandeep.

"So, who's going to go first?" Coach Joe asked gently, looking at the two boys.

"Jamie, left wing!" Jamie hopped from one foot to the other almost tripping over himself.

Coach Joe put his hands on Tandeep's shoulders and waited a moment for him to introduce himself. Tandeep raised his head up a bit, but not quite looking his Coach in the eye, then lowered his face to look at the ground without saying a word. He really wanted to speak, but the words just wouldn't come out.

"And this here is Tandeep and he's our right winger," Coach Joe finally said. "Now Ashleigh, it's your turn to say hi to the team."

With her smile now stretched even wider across her face Ashleigh said, "My name is Ashleigh. I'm from Hackney and I turned ten last week. I'm usually the striker or I play in midfield but I'm good in most positions and I'm really happy I made the team.

And just like that AC, an all-boys team, now had a girl. And not just any girl because Ashleigh was a very talented footballer. Suddenly, Shay felt his tummy tighten. Ashleigh played the same position as him, was fast, maybe even faster than him, and he had to admit she was good, really good. He couldn't quite believe this was happening, that she was actually on the team.

CHAPTER 6

Ashleigh

When Coach Joe spoke to Coach Kaan and Ashleigh about shin pads, Hassan kissed his teeth and mumbled under his breath, "Striker, yeah? She's never taking my spot."

"*But I'm good in most positions,*" Troy mocked, repeating what Ashleigh had just said, in a whispered, high-pitched voice.

Troy and Hassan sniggered under their breath, not wanting Ashleigh or their coach to hear how rude they were being or how they really felt.

"Right then, introductions are done," Coach Joe said looking around to make sure. His gaze stopped on Oscar. "Oscar your hair's all gone; I can only imagine that you've sacked your barber."

"Sorry Coach but jokes are my job if you don't mind," Oscar replied.

Coach Joe laughed in response. "Can you all start warming up? Start with a jog around the pitch together."

"I don't care what anyone says, girls are not as good as boys at football and that's a fact," Troy insisted as they walked down the pitch. He wasn't bothered whether Ashleigh could hear him or not.

"My cousin Angel's a girl and she's a really good player," Frankie said as he began to jog.

"Some girls are good, but not as good as me!" Oscar said.

Frankie noticed Ashleigh jogging towards them, and he would hate for her to hear what some of the boys were saying. "Troy and Oscar stop being so mean!" he hissed.

Troy rolled his eyes in response.

The team jogged on ahead leaving Ashleigh by herself. Shay looked over his shoulder at Ashleigh and noticed the smile had disappeared from her face. He deliberately slowed down to wait for her. Even though he wasn't thrilled that she was here, he hated seeing people left out. Shay motioned with his head for her to jog alongside him, and as she did, a little smile of relief at not being *completely* left out crept onto her face.

"Were you with another club before you came here?" Shay asked.

"Yeah, but I wasn't getting enough time on the pitch. My grandad knew about this club, so I thought I'd give it a go," Ashleigh replied.

"How long have you been playing?" Shay asked.

"Since I could walk really. I love it!" Ashleigh said, the smile returning to her face.

Shay took a deep breath before he finally asked Ashleigh the question he really wanted to know. "What position do you want to play in?

Ashleigh shrugged. "I like midfield or striker, but I honestly don't mind. I just want to be in a good team."

Shay nodded and wondered where the Coaches would play her and if she would take his position as striker.

"You lot need to move it, move it, move it!" Coach Joe rapped, and the under-tens picked up the pace.

Coach Kaan began the session with a bleep test. Everyone stood on the line and bent forward, then when he blew the whistle, everyone started running.

"Blessing, get a move on!" Coach Kaan hollered. "Come on, close the gap and beat that bleep!"

Blessing was too tired to answer! The players raced backwards and forwards across the pitch trying to beat the bleeps, many of them loudly huffing and puffing.

Coach Kaan shook his head.

Frankie and Hassan were at the front, way ahead of everyone else. Shay, Ashleigh and Tandeep were behind. Shay hoped Hassan wouldn't be as competitive towards Frankie as he had been last season.

Most of the players managed the first few bleeps before they came to a slow stop and dropped to the ground. Blessing was the first to time out.

"Guys, we need to work on your fitness!" Coach Joe bellowed across the pitch.

Like the others, Shay was exhausted and needed a puff of his inhaler. He now regretted spending so much time playing games online instead of playing real football. He came to a stop breathing hard. Only

Tandeep, Frankie, Ashleigh and Hassan were still running.

Not too long after, the bleep caught out Tandeep, Ashleigh and Hassan. A very triumphant Frankie threw his tired arms up in the air. Annoyed at not being the last one standing, Hassan stormed off sulking.

"Oi, there will be none of that this season," Coach Joe yelled at him.

"Nice run Ashleigh," Oscar said still trying to catch his breath.

"For a girl, right?" Ashleigh replied, still annoyed that they'd all jogged off at the start and not tried to make her feel welcome. Oscar didn't respond but his face went bright red.

CHAPTER 7

Let's See What She's Made Of!

Coach Kaan led the conditioning training while Coach Joe observed the players. Blessing was partnered with Troy and every time he ran forwards and backwards everyone could hear Troy shouting, "Hurry up!" All of them were unfit but Blessing was *really* unfit. When Shay had first joined the team, he remembered Blessing was as fast as him.

After a quick water break, Maxwell practiced goalkeeper techniques with Coach Kaan while the rest of the team did skills training with Coach Joe. Coach Joe partnered Ashleigh with Hassan for a one-on-one tackling practice. There were no winners or losers, but it gave the players a chance to practice and the coaches the opportunity to advise on tactics.

"Stay within the circle of the pitch," Coach Joe instructed.

It wasn't long before Hassan and Ashleigh were head-to-head in a tackle. Both were determined to win the ball by trying to put themselves between each other and the ball, but Hassan managed to shove Ashleigh off and take possession. Ashleigh fell to the ground with a deep frown on her face, but she quickly jumped back up.

"Hassan, you can't push her like that!" Frankie snapped.

The coaches didn't say anything. They'd seen Ashleigh at the trials and felt confident in her abilities. They knew if anyone could handle Hassan it was her.

Shay and the others looked on with raised eyebrows, surprised at how rough Hassan was being. Hassan barged Ashleigh when she tried to go for the ball again. Frankie knew Hassan wanted to prove his theory that boys were better at football than girls, or at least that *he* was, and it was clear that he had no inten-tion of taking things easy on Ashleigh.

As the players looked on, Ashleigh ran at Hassan and slid across the ground taking the ball from under his foot. She held on to it between her boots. Hassan fell to the ground leaving Ashleigh with enough time to jump up and keep possession of the ball. Hassan clenched his fists, his face getter redder by the second but Coach Kaan blew the whistle before Hassan could do anything silly.

Shay couldn't deny that Ashleigh was clearly skilful and strong. Some of the players cheered for her but Shay didn't. It worried him how good she was.

Shay and Frankie were up next. Frankie was determined to win, but so was Shay. As the two players intensely battled for the ball, Hassan began to chant loudly, "Shay! Shay! Shay!"

Frankie tried to block out the sound of Hassan's voice and focus on the task but what he really wanted to do was shout back at Hassan to SHUT UP!

Coach Kaan beckoned Hassan over and he instantly fell quiet as he walked to him with his head down. As the battle for the ball continued, Frankie kicked the ball too hard, causing it roll out of the centre circle and he went to fetch it.

Frankie overheard Coach Kaan telling Hassan off. He hoped it wouldn't make Hassan's behaviour worse because he knew that Hassan would take it out on him. Once their one-on-one was over, Coach Joe called Troy and Blessing over for their turn. Shay reached for his inhaler – being unfit was making his asthma play up more than usual.

Next it was time to practice penalties.

"Frankie, you're up!" Coach Kaan said.

Frankie jogged into position and adjusted his glasses while Oscar rolled the ball over to him. Wearing his glasses made Frankie feel more confident because he could see the goal clearly. He ran up to the ball and kicked it straight through Maxwell's legs and into the back of the net!

"Great shot!" Coach Kaan roared.

"Nice one," Shay called, and everyone cheered.

Frankie punched the air. Taking penalties had been a worry for him, so to hit the back of the net was a great feeling. Ever since he had started wearing glasses things had literally started to look better for him. That had all been down to Coach Reece, who noticed a problem last season, so he suggested to Frankie's mum that she should get his eyes tested.

At first, Frankie had been worried about wearing glasses. He thought he would be teased or bullied, or they would keep falling off when he played football. None of that had happened. In fact, the sports strap kept his glasses firmly in place, which made playing football much easier. Although pleased with his performance, there was a niggling feeling in Frankie's mind that made him wonder if it was worth all the effort. He loved playing football, but he only wanted to play for AC. If he moved house, he would have to leave his team and friends behind. Just the thought of it made his heart break.

CHAPTER 8

Breaking News

The sound of the whistle signalled the end of the session. The team walked over to the side of the pitch and threw themselves to the ground. They were exhausted!

Coach Joe reminded the parents to help the children be as active as possible before dismissing them.

"Boys, I have to agree with your Coach. You two did spend a lot of time gaming over the summer," Joanne said as they walked to the car. Tina nodded in agreement.

"Yeah, I know, and I can feel how unfit I am," Shay admitted.

"We'll have to make more of an effort to get you both over to the park and off the sofa. In fact, it'll be good for all of us," Tina said. "Since I've had Sanchez, I haven't had much time for exercise, so this could be the excuse I need to get fit."

"Frankie we can get our bikes out and go for rides over the hills in the park!" Shay suggested. "I've hardly used my bike all summer. I wonder if my dad fixed my puncture?"

Shay turned to look at his friend and noticed Frankie was behind him, dragging his feet.

Frankie had deliberately slowed down, so he was away from their mothers, and Shay caught on and matched his pace.

"Frankie, you alright?"

"No, not really," Frankie said, keeping his voice low. "I have to tell you something."

"What is it?"

"You can't tell anyone," Frankie said sternly. "Promise me."

"Okay," Shay said slowly. "Promise."

"Well, I think I might be leaving AC . . ."

"What?" Shay shouted.

"Keep your voice down Shay. I overheard my parents talking about a new house."

"You're moving?" Shay froze. "Are you joking?"

Frankie shook his head and continued walking.

For a moment Shay was speechless as his head flooded with thoughts. *When? Where to? Why? Will I ever see you again? What will I do without you? This isn't fair!*

Catching up to Frankie, Shay said, "But you can't leave! You're my best friend. What about school? Would you have to change?" Shay asked.

"Probably. I can't believe they would do this to me!" Frankie cried.

"This is so unfair!" Shay threw his arm across his best friend's shoulder and sighed. "What are you gonna do?"

"What can I do?" Frankie asked. "They're the parents, so they're in charge!"

"Shall I speak to my mum and dad?" Shay asked. "Maybe they can persuade your parents to stay?"

"I don't think that will work. I'll speak to my parents but I'm just trying to prepare myself for the bad news first!"

For a moment the two friends looked at each other, neither wanting to say what they both were thinking — *what will we do without each other?*

Distracted by their thoughts, neither of them noticed the short, round man wearing a hard hat, high-vis vest, and rucksack full of survey pegs walk past them.

CHAPTER 9

No News Is Good News, Right?

Saturday morning couldn't come soon enough for Shay. He was up early and dressed in his red AC training kit.

"Where's your bag? Is it packed?" Joanne asked, her eyebrows raised.

"Yes Mum! I've got my inhaler and EpiPen in it."

"Jo, I double checked his bag last night. Everything's in there, so don't worry. You just go see your mum and tell her hello from us," Danny said winking at her. "Come on boys, let's go pick up Frankie."

Danny opened the back door of the car for Rayne to get in and Shay jumped in the front. It was a short ride to Frankie's house and Shay looked out of the car window to see if Frankie was on his doorstep waiting for them like usual.

"Do you think Tandeep will be partnered with you again?" Danny asked. "I remember he helped set up some of your goals last season."

"I hope so. Last season we were on fire. I think I'll partner with him at training today."

"But what about Frankie? He's your best friend and he's on your team now. Won't he be your partner?" Rayne asked.

Shay shrugged. "It depends on what position he's in and the plays the coaches get us to do."

And whether he's still on the team if he hasn't moved, he thought.

Frankie only lived a few doors away and as they pulled up outside his house, the front door was already open. Tina was standing in the doorway, and she waved at them with one hand, the other was holding baby Sanchez. "Frankie, come on, they're here!"

Frankie ran out of the door with a quick goodbye to his mum and got in the car.

Shay stared at his friend with wide eyes, waiting for him to say something before impatiently whispering, "Well, what did they say?"

"I haven't asked them yet," Frankie whispered back.

Frankie was too worried to ask. He was afraid they might say yes. He'd heard his Nan say so many times that, 'No news is good news,' so he decided he didn't want to hear any news!

Training was full on; the drills were intense, and the players had to focus and work hard, but Frankie found training difficult. With the move constantly on his mind he kept missing instructions and being in the wrong place. Coach Joe yelled at him to focus, and this made Frankie want to scream, '*I can't because my life's falling apart,*' but he didn't.

After the warm-up, Coach Joe had them doing one touch passes in pairs. This is when one player passes the ball to their partner who then kicks it between two cones with only one touch of the ball.

The players got into groups of four and stood in a square. Shay ended up in the same group as Ashleigh, which at first annoyed him but then he realised it could be a good opportunity for him to show her up and remind everyone, especially the coaches, how good *he* was. Just in case she was coming for his spot.

Shay had the ball first; he passed it Tandeep, who kicked to Ashleigh, who passed to Frankie, then the ball went back to Shay, and round it went again, all with only one touch of the ball. There was no time to stop the ball and place it ready for a shot – if a player did that it was called a 'bad touch'. If the ball ended up in the wrong direction, then that player would end up in the middle, with the other three players forming a triangle around them. The person in the middle would then need to pressure the other three in the group to win back the ball. Whoever they won the ball from must then go into the middle and try to win it back.

Whenever Shay pretended he was going to pass the ball to another person and passed it to Ashleigh, Ashleigh was always alert and passed it on. This annoyed Shay even more. Frankie couldn't focus and kept 'bad passing,' so he was in the middle more than anyone else. In fact, everyone except Ashleigh had ended up in the middle more than once and although no one said anything, it hadn't gone unnoticed by the players or the coaches.

Frankie sat away from the others during break time. His mind was going over and over what he'd heard his mum say to his dad, 'It's a really nice house Colin, with a bigger garden and four nice-sized bedrooms. It would be great for the kids.'

Great for what kids? he thought to himself. Just thinking about a new house, a new school, a new football team, and maybe a new best friend made Frankie's stomach ache.

"Frankie! Frankie? Hello earth to Frankie!" Shay called but Frankie ignored him. Shay went up to his face and yelled, "Hello?" which made Frankie jump.

"Oi! Stop it Shay, what's wrong with you?" Frankie yelled.

"What's wrong with *me*? What's wrong with you? I've been calling you. Break's over and Coach Joe's called us back," Shay said before walking over to the coaches.

With slumped shoulders and head down, Frankie let out a long sigh as he walked over to join the others. He hadn't meant to snap at Shay. The last thing he needed was for them to fall out. Picking up the pace he jogged over to find Shay, so he could apologise, because right now he really needed his best friend.

Shay caught Frankie's eyes, but he was still annoyed and turned away first.

Sheepishly, Frankie stood next to him and whispered, "Sorry, you took me by surprise. I was thinking about the move."

Shrugging his shoulders, as if to say *forget it*, Shay focused on what Coach Joe was saying. Frankie let out a long slow sigh as he turned to face Coach Joe.

> *"When we're playing ball, things can distract us,*
> *But a true Baller Boy will maintain the focus!*
> *If they're shouting your name, keep your eye on the game,*
> *Because your one true goal, is to maintain your aim!"*

Catching Frankie's eye, Shay smiled at Frankie, who returned it. It was hard to stay annoyed when Coach Joe rapped. Shay knew he shouldn't get upset with Frankie, especially because he knew how sad he was about the move. With his own worries about Ashleigh possibly taking his spot on the team, Shay realised he needed Frankie to talk to. If only he could admit how threatened he was by Ashleigh.

CHAPTER 10

The Local Legend

Shay was the first to notice Coach Reece walking across the pitch.

"Frankie, look!" Shay said nudging him.

Coach Reece was a local legend, and in his youth had been a skilful player, which earned him the nickname Baller Boy. Now, along with Coach Joe, he owned AC United Football club and coached the under four-teens team. He was wearing his trademark red sports top and black tracksuit bottoms. His presence alone seemed to encourage the players to play their best football. Everyone knew he regularly popped in during training or turned up at matches to speak to the coaches and see how the players were getting on.

Whenever they saw Coach Reece, the players tried to impress him. Everyone wanted to be the next Baller Boy.

"Oh, so that's Coach Reece," Ashleigh said staring at him with wide eyes. "My granddad told me that he used to train with my uncle years ago and he was one of the best local players."

Shay wondered if Ashleigh knew that Coach Reece only selected the best players from each team to be a Baller Boy . . . and if she was hoping to be chosen. The thought of having more competition made his stomach do a somersault.

Training resumed with a short match between the main team and the development squad, and as Shay made a run towards the goal, Tandeep lined him up and the ball flew straight into the net.

"Nice one guys!" Coach Reece yelled.

"Yeah, nice play," Ashleigh called out to the boys.

Tandeep and Shay high-fived each other. Shay glanced at Ashleigh and wondered if she wasn't bothered that Coach Reece had complimented him. From the other end of the pitch, Frankie looked on and sighed. He remembered last season how Tandeep and Shay had worked really well together. All Frankie wanted was to fit into the team as easily as Shay had.

Coach Reece stayed until the end of training and watched the game. As soon as Coach Joe blew the whistle, the players ran to the edge of the pitch for a drink and an end of training chat with their coaches.

"That was an impressive performance guys," Coach Reece said to Shay and Tandeep who grinned. "It was great teamwork and I'm hoping to see more of that in your games this season. You've got your first match in a trophy event coming up soon."

"Thanks Coach, we'll be ready!" Shay said, happy that he had been noticed.

Coach Reece kept his gaze on Tandeep who stayed quiet.

"Tandeep, are you ready to win some games this season?" Coach Reece asked gently.

With his head down and his cheeks beginning to feel warm, Tandeep gave Coach Reece a thumbs-up in reply, and Coach Reece smiled satisfied.

They were dismissed and Shay raced over to his dad, Rayne, and Frankie, who were waiting to hear what Coach Reece had said to them. With wide eyes and a huge smile, speaking way too quickly from excitement, Shay retold the whole conversation, tripping over his words. Frankie walked silently back to the car listening to Shay go on and on about impressing Coach Reece. He felt *sort of* happy for his friend, but he also wished that Coach Reece had noticed him too.

CHAPTER 11

Fitter And Faster

Parkfield Primary School was filled with the noisy chatter of children waiting for the whistle to blow to signal the start of the school day. Mrs Anderson, their former Year 4 teacher, and now deputy head, stood in the playground observing the children. She always had a smile on her face that showed the gap between her front teeth. She was dressed in a smart trouser suit, high-heeled shoes and wore stylish finger print glasses.

At exactly 8.45am, the sound of Mrs Anderson's whistle filled the air and Shay, Frankie, Hassan, and the rest of the children made their way to line up for assembly.

For a change, Mrs Anderson was joined by their P.E. teacher, Ms Flinn, who was tall and slim, and used to play professional netball for England. She stood at the front of the hall wearing her standard tracksuit, with her hair swept up in a high ponytail. They were showing a short video about a school in Hackney in London, where every morning before school started the children and staff walked, jogged, or ran a daily mile.

At the end of the film, lots of children began to whisper excitedly about the idea. Mrs Anderson put her hand up to silence them.

"A few mornings last week, I was out in the playground before school started and noticed that most of you came to school nice and early, then stood around chatting until the whistle was blown." Mrs Anderson looked around the hall. "Ms Flinn told me about the daily mile idea, and we thought we could introduce it to our school. We think it would be a much better use of our time and you would all benefit from getting fitter."

"Research also suggests that exercise not only makes us healthier but also improves our concentration, so it will help our learning too," Ms Flinn added.

"Which is why we would like to try this at our school. Who would like to join in?" Mrs Anderson smiled at them.

Shay and Frankie immediately looked at each other and nodded.

"Put your hand up if you'd be interested," Ms Flinn looked out at the sea of children sitting in front of her. Immediately, half of the school put their hand up including Frankie, Shay and Hassan.

"Good! Letters will be going home this afternoon, and we will begin first thing tomorrow morning," Mrs Anderson said enthusiastically.

*

The following morning, the playground was filled with eager children, staff and parents, who were participating in their daily mile. Frankie and his sister Katie, Shay and his brother Rayne, and Hassan and his twin sister

Bejna, jogged alongside many other children around the junior field. Hassan had shot off fast and was way out in front, as usual wanting to be one of the first to finish.

Frankie and Shay had begun by jogging alongside their siblings until Rayne and Katie spotted their own friends and went off with them.

"Race you to the end!" Frankie yelled as he shot off leaving Shay trailing behind.

"Whatever!" Shay called out unbothered as he continued to jog at a steady pace.

The daily mile seemed to be an enormous success.

"Well done, Frankie! You've been around five times and that's your mile done for today," Mrs Anderson said as she ticked his name off the register.

Frankie bent forward with his hands on his knees. He tried to catch his breath, so it took a moment for him to answer. "Thanks, Miss, for organising this. Our football coach said we need to get fitter, so this is really going to help."

"Oh, great! But maybe next time take it steady. It's not really a race, it's just to help you improve your fitness. Some of you took off like racehorses today," Mrs Anderson exclaimed.

Frankie nodded, as a great idea came to him. Maybe if he could get AC United to start the daily mile as part of their warm-up, it could just be what they all needed to get fit!

CHAPTER 12
The Big Idea!

Frankie ran over to the team who were waiting for training to start on Friday evening. He wanted to be the one to tell the others about his idea. Shay chased behind him, even though he knew he didn't have a chance of catching up.

"Guys, I've got an idea!" Frankie bellowed, grinning from ear to ear.

Frankie's excited entrance had its desired effect as the players stopped chatting and turned to look at him.

"At school we've started the daily mile, where every morning before school we have to jog for a mile. I was thinking that we should do it as a team."

"We can be fast like Usain Bolt!" Shay added as he skidded to a halt beside Frankie.

"Sounds good," Blessing said, and the others quickly agreed.

"When do we start?" Oscar asked.

"At the next training. We can come fifteen minutes earlier to run the mile?" Frankie suggested. "Some of the parents at school joined in with us so maybe our families can join in?"

"My mums will. They love all that keep fit stuff. Sometimes they put my baby sister in her buggy and take her jogging," Oscar said grinning at the thought.

"But you need to be here early Oscar," Troy said, and Oscar frowned at him. "Sorry but you and your mums are always late. By the time you get here we'll all be done."

"I think the daily mile's a good idea," Shay said quickly to avoid an argument between Oscar and Troy. "Plus, we're good at doing things together. Remember last season when we raised all that money and bought the mascot costume?"

"A mascot costume?" Ashleigh looked around the pitch as if expecting to see it. "Where's the mascot?"

"We haven't worked out who will be in the costume yet," Shay admitted. "We raised quite a lot of money and had some left over, so we're giving it to a charity called ACLT who helped my grandma when she was ill."

"Oh, sorry to hear that. Is she okay?" Ashleigh asked softly.

"She had a cancer in her blood called Leukaemia, but she's much better now," Shay replied. He didn't like thinking about his gran being ill, so was keen to change the subject. "Any other ideas?" he quickly asked.

"We could also try walking to school instead of going by car?" Maxwell suggested.

"And less time gaming and more time at the park?" Ashleigh added making the boys laugh.

"Less PlayStation? No way!" Oscar scoffed and Ashleigh scowled at him.

"I'll ask Jamie's mum if she can bring him early as well," Frankie said, knowing that Jamie probably wouldn't listen to him, but his mum might want him to be involved.

Jamie was rolling around on the damp grass nearby.

"Come on you lot! Two laps around the pitch – let's go!" Coach Kaan said, ready to get the session started.

*

Sitting on the grass at the end of training, listening to Coach Kaan give the team talk, Shay nudged Frankie and whispered, "I think we should tell the coaches what we're planning to do, so that they know how serious we are getting fit."

"Yeah, good idea," Frankie whispered back.

As soon as the team talk was over, Frankie went to talk to the coaches, while Shay and the rest of the team gathered their belongings.

"Coach Joe can I speak to you about something?" Frankie asked.

Coach Joe picked up the bags of equipment. "Ah Frankie, I've also been meaning to speak to you. You've been a bit distracted lately, is everything okay?"

"Erm yes . . . well no . . ." Frankie could feel the tears stinging his eyes. "We might be moving house and if we do then I'll have to leave AC."

"I see. Where are you moving to?" Coach Joe asked.

"I don't know yet, but I don't want to move or leave!" Frankie said, his voice cracked with emotion.

Coach Joe put his hand on Frankie's shoulder. "Frankie, you're a good player and we'd hate to lose you, but there are lots of good clubs out there that would love to have you on their team. The thought of change can be difficult, but I'm sure you'll soon settle in and make new friends. Try not to worry. If you need to talk, I'm always here, but also speak to your family because I'm sure they wouldn't want you to be worry-ing about anything, okay?"

Frankie wiped the tears from his face and thanked him before sharing about the plans for the daily mile.

"This sounds great! I'm proud of you for taking the initiative. I'll let all the parents know," Coach Joe said.

On the other side of the pitch, Shay was walking past Jamie who was doing kick-ups. "Jamie, do you want to come in early tomorrow to run a mile with us? We're working on our fitness."

Jamie continued his kick ups without stopping. Shay shrugged. *It was worth a shot,* he thought. But as soon as Shay turned to walk away, Jamie called out "Yep!"

Shay smiled, surprised that Jamie had answered. He was excited that everyone was committed to working together.

CHAPTER 13

Questions

"Ready boys?" Frankie's dad, Colin, asked as he opened the back door of his car to take them home. Frankie's heart began to race as he climbed into the car. He wanted to ask his dad about the move but what if he said that they were moving far, far away?

Shay noticed Frankie looking at the floor.

Maybe he needs some help? Shay thought.

"Uncle Colin, Frankie wants to ask you something," Shay said.

Frankie shook his head, but Shay whispered, "You've got this."

Frankie wished he was as confident as Shay. Nevertheless, he took a deep breath and asked, "Dad, why are we moving house? Because I heard you and mum talking about it and I really don't want to go. I don't want to change schools and I definitely don't want to leave AC!"

Colin stared at Frankie in the rear-view mirror with his eyebrows raised. "Blimey, Frankie, where did all that come from? I'm sorry you found out like that but yes, me and your mum are thinking about moving. We need a bigger place and the houses where we live are quite expensive, so we're looking around."

"But Dad, I don't want to move! I like our house and we don't need a bigger one. I've only just made the main team!"

Colin opened the glove compartment, fished out a tissue and passed it back to Frankie, who now had tears spilling out of the corners of his eyes.

"Me and mum don't want you and Katie to move schools, nor do we want you to leave your best friend or AC, but we do need to move. If we're lucky and we find something close enough then you won't have to make any big changes, but I can't promise that. Do you understand?" Colin asked gently.

Sniffling, Frankie nodded his head to show he understood.

"If you're ever worried about anything please talk to me or Mum. We don't want you worrying about anything, you hear me?"

"Yes Dad. So, we are moving but not too far, is that what you're saying?" Frankie asked between the sniffles.

"We will try to find something local, but I promise that from now on I'll make sure you know what's going on, okay?"

"Okay . . . but what happened to the house with the four bedrooms that you were talking about?" Frankie asked. "Was that close by?"

"Yes, but it sold to someone else, so we're still looking."

Relieved, Shay turned to look at Frankie, but he was looking out of the car window across the fields.

Shay followed his gaze and saw two adults wearing hard hats and high-vis waistcoats. They were huddled over a large sheet of paper. They then looked around the fields and pointed at the clubhouse and pitch. Another person was standing behind a tripod taking photos, while two others were measuring out the area using a laser tape measure.

"What are they doing?" Shay asked.

"Do you think Oscar was right? And they've come to check out buying our pitch?" Frankie.

Shay's eyes widened. "I thought Oscar was joking!"

"Dad, look," Frankie said when they stopped at a red light. He pointed to the group of people walking around the fields. "Oscar told us something about the fields being sold off to make space for houses."

"How on earth would Oscar know that?" Colin asked as he stared at the men through the window.

"Something's going on and we need to find out what it is!" Shay said.

"What are we gonna do?" Frankie asked.

"I don't know but we should pull over and go over there and ask them what they're up to."

"Oi you two, none of that. You can't just go talking to strangers and asking them questions," Colin said. The light turned green and they drove off.

"Oh, yeah you're right uncle Colin, silly idea," Shay said. Lowering his voice so only Frankie could hear,

Shay added, "First thing at training we'll ask Oscar to tell us again in detail what he heard and this time we need to listen!"

"Okay and let's not worry about it till then," Frankie suggested. "It's probably nothing."

Shay nodded in agreement, although his stomach felt twisted in knots.

CHAPTER 14

Something's Going On!

Shay persuaded his dad to bring him and Frankie to training early so they could talk to Oscar. As Danny pulled into the car park, Shay and Frankie looked around nervously. They had expected to find bulldozers ripping their clubhouse down and digging up the pitches, but there was no one there. The fields and clubhouse looked the same as always.

Frankie and Shay sighed with relief. Oscar was probably joking. The boys sat on the grass as they waited for the rest of the team to arrive.

"Any update on the house?" Shay asked. He picked up a blade of grass and twirled it in his hand.

"They've been looking at houses online, but so far

they haven't found anything they like," Frankie responded.

"Are they still looking in this area?"

"Yeah . . . but also Essex."

"Essex!" Shay exclaimed. "That's so far! My uncle lives there and it takes ages when we go to visit."

Frankie shrugged. It wasn't like there was anything he could do about it. In the distance, he could see the team making their way over to them, annoyingly Oscar was missing.

After they greeted each other, Shay asked if anyone had seen the men on the fields after the last training session.

"Yeah, I did, why? What's up?" Troy asked.

"We thought it could be people checking out the area to buy it," Frankie said. "They looked really serious with cameras and hard hats and tape measures. Remember what Oscar was saying?"

"I thought he was joking," Ashleigh said.

"We all did," Shay added.

"I take it he's not here yet?" Troy asked looking around the fields with a smirk.

"We'll have a long wait," Blessing said, crossing his arms over his chest. "You know he's always late."

"We might as well get on with our daily mile while we wait," Shay suggested. "Jamie, you coming?" Shay called out to him.

Jamie had been sitting quietly with Kathy for a change reading a book about birds. He nodded at Shay and handed the book to his mum before he jogged over to his friends, adding in two cartwheels along the way.

"So, how far is a mile and when do we know if we've done it?" Blessing asked. The thought of jogging a mile worried him.

"My watch has a pedometer on it that can tell me the distance," Hassan said. He held up his arm showing off his latest new watch to Shay and Frankie. "We can use it to keep track of our mile."

"That won't work because everyone runs at different paces," Frankie said.

"Yeah but . . ." Hassan began but Shay interrupted him.

"Frankie's right. How about we run in separate groups or pairs so we can encourage each other?" Shay said.

"How about Frankie just runs by himself?" Hassan glared at Frankie. "All the way to Timbuktu and stay there!"

"Why are you always trying to start something with me?" Frankie snapped.

"What you gonna do about it?" Hassan asked, as he squared up to him.

"Hassan, just stop it," Shay said. He stood between them. "Frankie ignore him, we've got better things to do."

Hassan mumbled something under his breath and Frankie rolled his eyes in response.

"The point of this it to get fitter. It's not a competition." Shay gave a stern look to Hassan who crossed his arms. "At school everyone runs at different paces, and it takes the slowest people maybe fifteen minutes. I guess if we run for at least fifteen minutes then that's a mile or so."

Everyone agreed and started to jog. Hassan, who was again trying to encourage the others to stick with him, went up front, raising his arm in the air to show off the watch again.

With arms and legs flying everywhere the under-tens sprinted as fast as they could, most of them trying their best to outrun each other, despite Shay reminding them that it was *not* a competition. Hassan, Frankie and Ashleigh were way out in front, with Blessing at the back and everyone else in between. After the first lap the team began to slow down and jog, but not Hassan, of course he was determined to win.

"Come on, let's just keep going till we get to wherever Hassan stops. If he's using his watch that's probably the mile marker," Shay called out to the others.

Frankie, Ashleigh and Tandeep ran ahead just behind Hassan with Shay, Maxwell and Jamie behind them, while Troy and Blessing decided to walk the rest of the mile at the back before suddenly stopping altogether.

"Oh, come on!" Shay called, disappointed that they were giving up.

Frankie decided to run back to encourage Troy and Blessing. They eventually decided to jog the last twenty-five metres. Blessing picked up the pace and jogged on with Frankie leaving Troy behind.

As Frankie and Blessing approached the end of the mile the others clapped and cheered for them. Although out of breath, Blessing finished with a massive smile on his face.

CHAPTER 15

Spill The Beans!

The team collapsed on the ground, exhausted from their run.

"Hey guys," Oscar said brightly as he joined them. "What did I miss?"

"You're late and you missed the mile!" Ashleigh said.

Without giving Oscar a chance to respond, Shay asked, "Remember you told us about the fields being sold off? Can you tell us again?"

"Oh sure. My neighbour said that the council want to sell the pitches and club and use the space to build houses." Oscar frowned. "Why?"

"Well, after training we saw some people checking out the clubhouse and we think it was about the sale,"

Frankie explained. "They were taking pictures and measuring up."

"What else did your neighbour say?" Shay asked.

"That was it. She said if she heard anything else she would tell my mums." Oscar replied. "But I haven't heard anything since."

Shay groaned. "How can we find out for sure what's going on?"

"My neighbour works for the council so I can ask if she knows anything else?" Oscar suggested.

"Yeah, good idea, thanks Oscar," Shay said.

The coaches arrived and the team slowly walked over to meet them, but they quickly were on high alert when they saw Coach Reece appear from the car park. All thoughts about the visitors and the sale temporarily went out of their heads. Their only thought was to impress him.

With Coach Reece watching, training got off to a good start – everyone was doing their best in the warm-up. Next, Coach Kaan partnered them up and Shay was placed with Ashleigh. He couldn't hide his surprise.

Why would they put me with her? he thought.

"Shay, are you ready?" Ashleigh asked, keen to get started on their one-touch lateral passes.

"I guess," Shay mumbled. He wished he was partnered with anyone else but her.

Ashleigh rolled Shay the ball to start. She was on her toes ready. Shay kicked the ball to the right of her and she shuffled across, stopped it and passed it straight back, he went left, and she returned it. He tried to dummy right but she was focused, each time she shuffled across and passed it back to him. Her accuracy was perfect. Shay's tummy filled with knots.

"Nice movement and passing Ashleigh. Well done, keep it up!" Coach Reece shouted.

"Thanks Coach," Ashleigh called back, without missing a pass.

Shay heard the comment and the knots in his stomach tightened. Ashleigh was good and now Coach

Reece was noticing. Shay sighed, now really worried about being replaced by *her.*

After the whistle had been blown, Coach Reece called the parents over to join them.

"Morning everyone, before you leave, I'd like a few minutes of your time," Coach Reece said, as everyone gathered around. "Firstly, well done, I've been hearing great things about your extra fitness training so keep it up. The coaches will do everything to support you *and* I've been hearing that some parents have been joining in to support you as well."

"Yeah, mine and Frankie's mums," Shay said.

"That's great and all of the support is appreciated. The rest of you are welcome to join in too," he added, looking around and grinning at the parents as they tried to avoid his eyes. "As you know, we have a match next Saturday! It'll be the first trophy event, so we need you all match fit, and working together as a team. Next week, we'll let you know who you'll be against."

"Yes!" the players shouted, excited to play their first trophy match as under-tens.

Shay wondered what position the coaches would play Ashleigh in and he prayed it wouldn't be in his position as striker.

Although anxious about moving, Frankie tried to put it out of his mind and focus on the game ahead.

Stepping forward, Coach Kaan yelled, "Good session today everyone! I'll put all the details for the match next week in the WhatsApp group. I expect you to all be there and on time. Hands in."

The team placed their hands in the middle one on top of another.

"3-2-1!"

"UNITED!" the players shouted back.

CHAPTER 16

Win or Lose

The first match was always exciting. The Football Association allowed under-tens to play in up to three trophy events during the season, lasting a maximum of four weeks each. These short-term experiences were designed to help children learn about winning and losing in an appropriate environment.

The Mighty Lions came out of the AC United clubhouse dressed in their bright yellow kit. Frankie hoped he would be starting the match and was disappointed when Coach Joe didn't put him straight on. Being a substitute wasn't quite what he'd hoped for, but he knew he'd get on at some point, so he had to stay positive. Shay was relieved to find himself in his usual position as striker. Ashleigh was on the subs bench with Frankie.

Pete, the AC club secretary, was the match commentator for their home game against The Mighty Lions. The opposing team were undeniably fitter, faster, stronger, and immediately took charge of the game.

"And that was a stinger of a goal by The Mighty Lions' Emilio!" Pete roared into the microphone as The Mighty Lions fans cheered. "Look at AC striker Shay running down the middle, with the two Lions' defenders ready to take him on. He's looking around for someone to pass to, but where's the rest of his team?"

Having no choice, Shay took the shot, but it was blocked by Casio, the Lions' defender, who sent the ball back in the direction of the AC goal. It wasn't long before there was another goal from the Lions' Emilio – his second of the match.

"Come on you lot, mark up!" Shay yelled, annoyed at conceding a second goal.

When it came to skill, AC were great on the ball. Their passing and dribbling were both tight, and their tackling was on par, but as soon as the Lions got the ball and made runs with it, AC found they could barely keep up with them!

"That's a great bit of tackling from AC's Jamie, who passes the ball to Shay, but the kick's too long and Shay isn't able to stop it. Now the ball's out of play," Pete said.

"Unlucky AC, keep going!" shouted someone from the crowd.

"Ref, sub please. Shay!" Coach Joe said. Shay jogged towards him confused, wondering why his coach was calling him over. Coach Joe patted him on the back and said, "Good game Shay! Okay, Ashleigh, you're on."

Shay jogged towards the bench. He couldn't believe he had been subbed for Ashleigh! With clenched teeth and his fists in tight balls, Shay almost threw himself onto the bench. He put his hands on his head and kept his eyes to the ground, not wanting to look at anyone. He couldn't understand what had just happened.

Why have I been taken off? That had never happened before unless he'd been injured.

"Shay, you alright?" Frankie asked. He tried to comfort his friend by putting his hand gently on Shay's back.

By half time the score remained steady at 2-0 to The Mighty Lions, who ran off the pitch looking pleased with themselves. AC on the other hand walked off with their heads down, already feeling defeated.

"Right, come on guys, you know what you need to do," Coach Joe said. "When the Lions have possession, Blessing and Troy, you must defend our goal and help

Maxwell keep those balls out. Wingers – Jamie and Tandeep – I need you to push forward and get the ball across to the guys in the middle. Ashleigh and Hassan, you need to push forward and let off more shots. Don't keep the ball too long and don't allow their defenders to tackle."

"Yes, Coach Joe," Ashleigh said, already on her feet, raring to get back on the pitch.

"Teamwork is what you need today guys. Come on, keep your heads up."

Shay sat with the team for the half-time talk without saying a word, but in his heart, he felt that if he had stayed on, AC would have scored.

CHAPTER 17

You'll Come Back From This!

"Look at Hassan, the AC skipper, making a run for goal, but The Mighty Lions defenders are hot on his heels," Pete said into the microphone.

Hassan's elbow caught Emilio on the back of the head. Emilio pushed him back in retaliation. Suddenly, they were squaring up to each other until the ref blew the whistle and separated them.

Coach Joe turned to Frankie and said, "Frankie, warm up, you're going on."

Frankie jumped to his feet then looked at Shay who gave him a thumbs-up but could barely mange a smile.

After a few minutes, Coach Joe held his hand up

and called out to the ref, "Ref, sub please, Hassan!" and waved Hassan over to him.

Running on to the pitch, Frankie was determined to help his team. He didn't look at Hassan or touch palms with him because he knew Hassan wouldn't want him to.

Although Frankie was fast and good down the centre, The Mighty Lions always seemed to push back and take control of the match.

"The Mighty Lions are keeping the AC defence under pressure, and this could be dangerous for AC, but Troy's fast and is managing to block those thunder shots! Troy has managed to win the ball and has passed it to Frankie, who's charging down the centre of the pitch. With seconds to go, he needs to take the shot or pass it up front, what will he do? He shoots . . . oh no, he's too far out and misses. Unlucky Frankie!" Pete said sympathetically.

Frankie couldn't believe he'd missed. Not wanting anyone to see his disappointment, he threw his hands onto his head and squeezed his elbows together, hiding his face.

Ashleigh rushed over to him and patted him on the back, "Good try mate, unlucky," she said softly.

By the end of the match, when Pete yelled out the final score, AC were hardly listening. They already knew the score and *definitely* didn't need Pete to remind them of their 2-0 loss to The Mighty Lions. However, win lose or draw, AC knew they had to be good sports. So, when Coach Joe told them to, the whole team, including Shay, lined up and shook hands with The Mighty Lions and congratulated them on their win.

"Keep your heads up," Coach Kaan said to AC. "You haven't played to the best of your ability, and I think you know that, but don't worry you'll get them next time. What can we improve on for the next match?"

"I should have tried to shoot more and look out for someone to pass to," Shay admitted. Although disappointed with the team's loss, Shay was relieved that Ashleigh hadn't scored either. Maybe her taking his spot was just a one off.

"I think we needed to get into positions ready to take a pass or call for the ball, then we could have helped more," Ashleigh said.

Exactly, then maybe I would have been able to score and stay on, Shay thought.

"We could've done better man-to-man marking with the faster attackers, but we couldn't keep up with them," Troy said.

"You should have kept me on!" Hassan snapped.

The coaches looked at one another but didn't say anything to him.

"You know what you need to do next time. We'll come back from this," Coach Kaan said. "Right, come on everyone, right hand in, ready . . . 3-2-1-"

"UNITED!" they chorused, as they threw their hands in the air, but Shay's heart wasn't in it. Losing was definitely not fun.

"Enjoy the rest of your day and see you at training on Friday," Coach Joe said.

CHAPTER 18

A New Captain

"Shay and Hassan, can we have a quick word before you go?" Coach Joe asked.

Shay and Hassan shared a confused look with each other before they walked over to where Coach Joe, Coach Kaan and Coach Reece were standing.

"We wanted to talk to you about the role of team captain," Coach Joe explained. "As you know it's about being a leader, supporting and motivating your team. Shay, we've been watching you and we'd like to offer you the chance to captain the team."

Shay couldn't believe they were asking him! "Yes please!"

"What?" Hassan yelled. "But I'm the captain!"

Startled by Hassan's reaction, Shay gasped. He understood that Hassan was upset but shouting at the coaches was taking it a step too far.

"Hassan, the way you're behaving right now is one of the reasons we've had to ask you to stand down," Coach Joe explained. "You can't keep losing your temper when things don't go your way."

"But this isn't fair!" Hassan argued.

"Hassan, that's our final decision. Now boys, shake hands. We need you working as a team," Coach Kaan said.

"I'm the *best* captain this team will ever have. You wait till I tell my dad!" Hassan shouted. He stormed off without shaking Shay's hand.

As the coaches followed Hassan over to speak with his dad, Shay ran to tell his dad and Frankie the good news. He was so excited; it took him ages to get the words out.

"That's great son, well done! You deserve it and I think you're a great leader," Danny said. He held out his fist and Shay fist-bumped him.

Frankie walked to the car with a sinking feeling in his stomach. He was fed up with good things always happening to Shay. He sighed heavily as he fought back the tears.

Shay didn't notice that Frankie hadn't said anything. Instead, he spent the entire journey home talking about being made captain. "I wasn't expecting it; I can't believe they chose me!"

I was starting to worry that they wanted to replace me with Ashleigh, but this must really mean they still think I'm good, Shay thought, his smile growing even wider.

Frankie, now in a world of his own, wasn't listening because he was too busy thinking about all the things around him that were changing including Shay being made captain. Deep down, he knew Shay deserved it and that he was a born leader, he just wished he would get these opportunities as well.

"Frankie? Hello? Earth to Frankie!" Shay said waving his hand in front of Frankie's face to get his attention.

"What? Oh, sorry, I was just thinking about our next match," Frankie lied.

"Are you worried about it?"

"No, not really . . . maybe a little bit. I just want to do well," Frankie said.

"Frankie, we're a team. We all want to do well and if we do what we've been practicing then we stand a good chance of winning. When you get in let's play FIFA."

"Yeah, if I'm allowed, but I don't think I will be," Frankie lied again.

Frankie knew his mum would let him go online, but he wasn't in the mood. He knew that Shay was just being a good friend and he knew that he should congratulate him, but the more he thought about Shay being made captain the more his heart raced, and his tummy tightened. No, he *definitely* wasn't in the mood.

When Danny's car pulled up outside his house, Frankie leapt out of the car.

"Thanks Uncle Danny, bye."

Danny always walked Frankie safely to his door and often stayed to chat with Frankie's dad Colin, his old school friend. "Frankie, wait up. I'll walk you in. What's the rush?"

"Oh sorry, nothing, I'm just a bit tired. I'll walk on and you can watch me from there." Frankie quickly walked to his front door without another word.

"See you later Frankie!" Shay waved but Frankie didn't stop to look back or answer.

That's weird, Shay thought.

Without taking his eyes off Frankie, Danny watched as the front door opened and his dad Colin stuck his head out. Danny gave him a thumbs-up.

"Frankie seemed a bit odd, didn't he?" Danny said to Shay. "He didn't congratulate you on being captain."

"I did think he was acting weird," Shay said. "He didn't even say bye."

"Frankie's obviously got a lot going on. He could be moving, leaving AC, and you lot have another match coming up. Maybe he's feeling overwhelmed? You just carry on being his friend and I'm sure everything will sort itself out."

"Yeah, thanks Dad you're probably right," Shay said as he thought about what his dad had just said.

But I'm really proud that I've been made captain especially because I was worried about losing my place. I want to share it with Frankie like we usually share everything. Why are things changing?

CHAPTER 19

The All-Stars Cup

The following Saturday, it began to drizzle as AC United and their families made their way across Wellington Park towards the pitch. After their recent defeat, AC felt they had something to prove and desperately wanted to win.

Shay noticed Hassan was unusually quiet and thought he must still be annoyed at losing the captaincy. Hassan had been benched for his rudeness to the coaches and Frankie was delighted to be in the starting line-up.

Coach Ryan, a coach and parent from The Essex Road Giants, also known as ERG, was commentating this match. ERG won last season's All Stars Cup and were going to be tough to beat.

"AC's Shay and Tandeep are using their pace and power to good effect which is unsettling the ERG rearguard," Coach Ryan said. "But ERG have started to dominate the ball, showing their experience and quality. Wow, good combination play in midfield by ERG's Alexia and Del, which has opened up the game. A quick, incisive through ball by the ERG winger has found their midfielder. AC's Blessing is trying to keep up, Maxwell's trying to get the ball of Alexia and it's . . . a goooooal! Alexia's brilliantly executed lob over Maxwell was class; 1-0 to the Essex Road Giants!"

AC hung their heads already looking defeated. Alexia was showing up their entire team.

"AC have started making inroads and are back in the game . . ."

Shay and Alexia were both going for the ball, determined to win it. As the ball got away from them, Shay and Alexia ran after it, but she slid on the grass to catch the ball with her foot and missed. She caught Shay hard on the ankle, which brought him down to the ground.

Shay stood up. He hoped to shake it off, but the sharp pain in his ankle caused him to wince and limp. He could not believe he had picked up an injury on his first game as captain.

He noticed Ashleigh warming up on the side and he knew she would be taking his place as striker. This made him feel even worse than the injury. Hobbling off the pitch, Shay gave Ashleigh a weak high-five as she took his place, and Troy was put in place as captain.

Frankie charged past two ERG players with the ball and none of them stood a chance of catching up. Frankie looked around for someone to pass to and spotted Ashleigh in the clear, holding her hand up to let Frankie know she was ready for the pass. Frankie crossed the ball to Ashleigh who did a perfect overhead kick, which sent the ball into the top corner of the net. Ashleigh jumped for joy at her goal, as Frankie and the others ran over to pat her on the back and congratulate her.

"Thanks Frankie, that was a great assist," Ashleigh beamed.

"Teamwork makes the dream work," Frankie replied.

"Great goal!" Coach Ryan said. "Looks like AC have found their flow and have started taking the fight to ERG."

Ashleigh won the ball twenty yards from goal and played a great one-two with Tandeep.

"With moves like that, I think she's gonna be one to keep an eye on!" Coach Ryan said.

"Ashleigh! Ashleigh!" the AC fans chanted.

Every time he heard her name, Shay's stomach tightened and twisted in knots.

Ashleigh went for goal again, but her shot was blocked by the goalie. In that moment Shay would have preferred AC to lose rather than *her* score the winning goal.

CHAPTER 20

The Green-Eyed Monster!

The half-time whistle went, and AC brought Jamie on to replace Oscar. Frankie was pleased that he was staying on for the second half. Now he had more time to impress the coaches, but he felt sorry for Shay who was sitting on the bench with his head down.

"My goodness, this second half is proving to be a real battle!" Coach Ryan said. "Look at the ERG midfielder Alexia. She's managed to get away from the AC defence and her efforts have been parried brilliantly by the ERG winger, but the follow-up effort has gone wide. Unlucky, really unlucky, and it's a corner!"

"Mark up!" Blessing shouted to the team encouraging them to mark their opponents closely, not wanting ERG to get close to scoring again. "And mark Alexia better."

ERG took the corner; it fell to ERG's winger Ben whose curling effort kissed the post and went wide, and thankfully was cleared by Troy.

The AC fans sighed with relief. It was down to the last few seconds of the match and one last final chance to score. The ERG captain went for a goal, but Maxwell was alert and headed it away. It was a missed opportunity by ERG and a massive relief to AC.

The final whistle signalled a draw and the season officially on. AC United Player of the Match was given to Ashleigh, who found herself surrounded by her teammates cheering and applauding. Shay stood to the side of the crowd.

A relieved and sweaty team gathered around Coach Reece who was smiling with pride at his players. "Congratulations and a great team effort today. If you continue playing like this, you'll be in with a chance of winning some trophies this season!" The players grinned from ear to ear. Because he didn't finish the match, Shay felt Coach Reece's comments didn't really apply to him. He didn't feel like part of the team.

"Great work Ashleigh," Coach Reece said, and Ashleigh beamed back.

It took all of Shay's effort not to roll his eyes.

"Alexia is a wicked player, isn't she?" Troy said. "But not as good as Ashleigh."

"Oh, so now you're saying girls can be good players?" Ashleigh asked and Troy looked sheepishly back at her.

"Come on, obviously girls can play as good as boys!" Coach Joe said. "Some are even better. Ashleigh is a real asset to us and we're lucky to have her."

Shay had heard enough of Coach Joe and the others gushing over Ashleigh. He went to stand beside Frankie. Right now, he needed his best friend.

"Frankie, you were brilliant today. Great game," Shay said, putting his arm around his shoulders.

"Thanks Shay! I loved every minute of it. Sorry you got injured, but you know what, Ashleigh did well stepping in for you, didn't she? I think she's a great striker."

Shay stared at Frankie with wide eyes. *Was Frankie comparing me to Ashleigh?*

"That's my position!" Shay said. He pulled his arms away and Frankie frowned. "Why would you say that? Some friend you are, I hope you do move far away."

"Shay, I didn't mean it like that," Frankie said. "I just meant she's a good player. I'm sorry that I upset you." Shay began to limp away, and Frankie followed him. "Slow down or you might make your ankle worse."

"What do you care?" Shay spun around and glared at Frankie, which made him stop in his tracks. "I'm sure you'd be happy to replace me with Ashleigh anyway."

"That's not true!" Frankie insisted, but Shay turned his back on him.

Frankie sighed, wondering if this time he'd really messed things up between them.

CHAPTER 21
What The Papers Say

"You lot are doing well, aren't you?" Danny said to Shay, as they sat around the table eating dinner. "In eight weeks, you've only lost one game."

"Thanks Dad!" Shay forked the last of his dinner into his mouth. "Mum, dinner is so nice. Can I have a bit more chicken please?" Shay licked his fingers.

"I'll second that. Can I have some more rice and peas please?" Danny asked.

"And me three. Can I have more of everything please? Except the carrots?" requested Rayne.

As Joanne got up from the table, she looked at her *three boys* and laughed. "Yes, to all, but you lot are doing the washing up. I'm having what's left of today off to plait my hair! Sunday should be my rest day."

After dinner, Shay and Danny tidied up the kitchen while Joanne sat in the living room helping Rayne finish his homework while she undid her plaits. As Shay and Danny entered the living room, Shay noticed the computer screen flashing.

"Dad, can I go online for a bit? Blessing's inviting me into a game?"

Danny looked at his watch. "Sure. You can do one hour. It'll give me a chance to do a bit of one-on-one with Rayne in the garden once he's done his homework."

Shay logged on and was soon lost in the moment as he played FIFA with Blessing. Before he knew it his mum was calling him to do his homework. Reluctantly, Shay said goodbye to his mate and joined his mum in the living room who had his homework folder open.

"Right, let me see, your topic is to read and write a newspaper report and today you need to read a variety of reports," Joanne said sitting on the sofa. "Go and get the newspaper that came through the letterbox on Friday. It's in the hallway."

Shay got the paper and laid it on the floor. He turned straight to the sports section at the back, scanning the pages. Clearing his throat like a grown up, he read an article about a player that had just been bought for millions of pounds. "Imagine getting paid millions of pounds to do something you love!"

That'll be me soon, Shay thought to himself.

Next, he turned to the front page, flicked through the pages and noticed a picture of a squirrel with the headline:

Tips to encourage more wildlife during spring

Shay continued to flick through the pages when Joanne suddenly put her hand between the pages to stop him from turning the page. "Hang on a minute, love."

She pulled the newspaper closer and began to read to herself. Joanne's jaw dropped. "Danny, come here! You're not gonna believe this!"

"What is it, Mum?" Shay asked as he tried to read over her shoulder. Danny walked into the room, meeting Joanne's eye's that were wide with concern.

In small writing there was a notice in the planning section from the local council.

"Marshals playing fields, clubhouse and grounds: for sale," Shay read out.

Are they selling the land our club is on? Does that mean AC will close? Where will we train? What are we going to do!?

With all the unanswered questions spinning around in his head, Shay burst into tears.

CHAPTER 22

For Sale

Shay had hardly slept. He had tossed and turned all night, thinking of AC United being forced to close.

"Mum, are you ready? I need to tell Frankie about what's happening to AC."

The fallout with Frankie was already forgotten.

"Shay, calm down. Rushing into school isn't going to change anything. You'll see Frankie in a bit and Dad said he'd try to find out more about the sale of the club." Joanne sighed. "Stop worrying until we know what's happening, okay?"

Shay tried but it was hard. He scraped his breakfast into the bin unable to eat it.

As soon as Shay saw Frankie in the school playground, he hurried over, concern written all over his face.

"Did you hear? The council is selling off AC's ground, so Oscar was right," Shay said. "Look, I tore this out of the newspaper."

"I can't believe it!" Frankie said as he took the newspaper clipping from Shay.

Hassan walked over to Shay and Frankie with his usual confident smirk on his face. He was carrying a new football under his arm.

"Have you seen this?" Shay asked pointing at the newspaper clipping.

Frankie held the clipping out to Hassan. Without even looking at it, Hasan swallowed hard and shook his head, hoping they wouldn't expect him to read it. "Yeah, my mum told me yesterday."

Hassan had dyslexia and couldn't read very well; he was embarrassed by this and didn't want his friends to know. Even though they were in the same class, he thought he had managed to keep it from them. He always managed to find a way to get out of reading and even when he had no choice, his teacher was really good at supporting him. As far as he was aware at school only his teacher, teaching assistant and sister knew about his dyslexia but in reality, the whole class knew he didn't read very well, and none of them were the slightest bit bothered by this.

"Got to go, see you in the pitch," Hassan said before he jogged off.

"Well, he might not be bothered but we are. We need to figure something out. How do we save our club?" Shay asked Frankie.

"I don't know but we'll work it out . . . and Shay?" Frankie took a deep breath. "I'm sorry about the other day. Of course, Ashleigh can never take your place and I'm sorry you got injured. I'm glad to see you're not hobbling today."

"Thanks Frankie. I know Ashleigh's good and when she came on as a sub in my place, I was really worried about her taking my spot," Shay admitted. He realised this was the first time he had ever said it out loud. He knew he was intimidated by how good Ashleigh was.

"Sorry Shay, I didn't realise," Frankie said. "I've got some news though."

"Oh no, what is it?" Shay couldn't take any more bad news.

"My parents have found a house and we're going to look at it."

"What? Where is it?"

"Kent!" Frankie said sadly.

"Kent! Where's that? It sounds far."

"It is. I'll have to change school *and* football team."

"But I thought your dad said he would try to stay local? I hope they don't like it, in fact I'm gonna pray they don't like it!" Shay declared. He closed his eyes.

"We're going to see it on Thursday, but I already know I'm going to hate it," Frankie said. "I just don't wanna move. I wish all these things selling and changing would just go away and leave us alone!"

"Yeah, tell me about it. We can't do anything about your house move, but we have to do something about this!" Shay said tapping the newspaper cutting. "The question is . . . what?"

*

On Friday evening Frankie got in the car with his football bag and sat next to Shay.

"How was the house?" Shay asked.

"My parents didn't like it."

"Yes!" Shay said and Frankie gave him a fist bump.

The Friday evening traffic through North London was surprisingly light and Joanne managed to get the last parking spot nearer to the clubhouse instead of where they usually parked close to the side gates.

They waved goodbye and prepared to walk past the clubhouse over to the pitch but as they got closer Shay and Frankie noticed that on the wall above the window of the clubhouse, a large For Sale sign was attached to it.

"It's really happening!" Shay cried. "What are we going to do?"

For Sale
Marshalls
playing fields
and
clubhouse

"Let's see if everyone else knows. I think the mile is gonna have to wait today."

Shay and Frankie ran over to the pitch where the rest of AC United were. Oscar, as usual, was running late and Hassan was absent.

"We need to show you something!" Shay shouted. He gestured at them to follow him.

"Guys, we've got a big problem," Frankie said as they ran back towards the clubhouse.

"What?" Maxwell asked.

"Look!" Frankie said as he pointed to the For Sale sign. "They're selling our club!"

CHAPTER 23

Not On Our Watch!

The players gasped, staring up at the For Sale sign.

"When did this happen? It wasn't here last week?" Troy demanded.

"I can't believe Oscar was right!" Blessing said.

As the team stared at the sign, not knowing what to say or do, they didn't notice that the coaches and parents had gathered to join them.

"Right, can everyone listen for a minute please!" Coach Reece said and everyone turned to him. "As you can see, and we have only recently had it confirmed ourselves, the council is selling off the clubhouse and surrounding land to developers. We are really disappointed with the decision but there is nothing we can do. We will continue to train and play here and hope to find new premises for the club as soon as possible. It's already January and we hope to be able to finish the rest of the season here, so let's try to carry on as normal."

"Normal? How can we carry on as normal?" Maxwell wailed.

"New premises? We don't want new premises. We like it here!" Shay shouted.

"AC has been here for years so why should we have to go?" Frankie demanded. "They should find other land to build on."

"Yeah!" The players and parents agreed.

"If we see even one bulldozer, it'll be us versus them!" Shay declared defiantly.

"Unfortunately, there isn't anything we can do," Coach Joe said sadly. "But come on, we still have training to get on with and matches to play."

The team dragged their feet as they followed the coaches back to the pitch.

"We're not gonna just leave it there, are we?" Maxwell whispered to Shay.

"No way!" Shay said shaking his head.

"But what are we gonna do?" Maxwell asked.

"What can we do?" Troy frowned.

"I think we should contact the sellers and ask them how much it costs. Maybe we could all buy it?" Blessing suggested.

"Yeah, we could try and raise some money like we did last season," Troy said.

"I don't think we can raise enough to ever afford it. But we could tell them how unhappy we are and ask them not to sell it," Frankie suggested. "Maybe if they're nice they'll understand?"

"Do you think they would listen to us? We're only kids," Troy said scowling.

"I think we should at least try to make them listen," Shay said. "We need to do something."

Late as usual Oscar came running over. "I saw in the paper about our club. I told you but you lot wouldn't listen, they can't just sell it though, can they?"

"Sorry Oscar, now we know it's true," Troy said.

"We won't let them sell, not on our watch!" Shay said. "We need to think of ideas to try and stop them."

"We could do a demonstration. Everyone can walk through the streets holding up signs and banners saying, 'hands off our club!'" Oscar suggested.

"That's a good idea Oscar. We could also do a petition and get everyone to sign it," Ashleigh said.

Frankie noticed Tandeep wipe a tear away and Frankie put an arm around him.

"Don't worry, we won't let the club go without a fight! Are you in?" Frankie held out his fist and Tandeep bumped it with his own.

"Look, there's Hassan," Troy said.

Hassan and his dad were walking over to the coaches and the team were surprised to hear Hassan's dad raise his voice and point his finger at the coaches. He was speaking in Turkish, and Coach Kaan was going red in the face.

"Wow, I wonder what that's all about?" Frankie asked as Hassan and his dad walked back to their car without a backwards glance.

CHAPTER 24

Don't Get Your Hopes Up!

Hassan and his twin sister Bejna pulled up outside the school gates in their dad's huge, flashy, silver car and climbed out of the passenger door. They slammed the door shut and waved as the car pulled away. Shay looked over at them, eager to know why Hassan's dad had been shouting at the coaches. Frankie didn't really want to be around Hassan and was glad that he hadn't been at training, but he was curious to know what was going on.

They waited for Hassan to join them.

"What happened at training?" Shay asked.

"Me and my dad weren't happy when they took the captaincy away from me," Hassan explained. "After

I played well *and* with a good attitude at our last game, my dad asked if they were gonna make me captain again and they said no! So, my dad went mad and took me off the team." Hassan shrugged unbothered. "Anyway, I've joined a new team now."

"You've left AC already?" Frankie gasped. "What team have you gone to?"

"You'll have to wait and see!"

Shay couldn't believe that Hassan had really left them and in the middle of the season. Hassan was a massive asset to the team and him leaving would affect them all massively. Frankie on the other hand thought it was the best news she had heard all week.

At lunchtime, Shay and Frankie decided to talk to Mrs Anderson. The daily mile had been the perfect way for them to get fitter so maybe she would have some more advice on how to save their club. They knocked on the open door to her office and he spun herself around on her chair to face them with a big smile.

"Come in boys and have a seat. How can I help?"

Frankie and Shay explained all about the sale.

"I must say, I did hear about it. It's such sad news. Reminds me of when the local library was under threat of closure and some local people organised a petition to try and stop it."

"What's a petition?" Frankie asked. "One of the players mentioned it the other day."

"A petition is when you write a letter that gives a voice to an issue that matters to you. Then, you get everyone who agrees with you to sign it. After that, you take the petition to the local council and hope it helps to change their mind. It doesn't always work but it's worth a try," Mrs Anderson explained.

"We could do it Frankie," Shay said excitedly. "We could write about how much our club means to everyone and get people to sign it."

"Yeah! Let's do it. Thanks Miss," Frankie said feeling hopeful for the first time in ages.

CHAPTER 25

Music To Our Ears

"Why don't you and the team jog around the woodlands with me, Kathy and Jamie? We're going to do our miles," Joanne said to Shay as they walked towards the pitch.

"Miles?" Shay exclaimed. "You only have to do one!"

"We're taking our fitness very seriously," Tina said.

"Might be nice to have a change of scenery," Joanne added.

"Yeah, sounds good. I'll ask the others," Shay said.

The players chatted away as they stretched, warming up for their mile.

"Guys, have you heard about Hassan? He's left AC," Shay said.

He could tell they didn't know by their surprised expressions.

"For real?" Troy asked puzzled. "Why would he do that?"

"Because the coaches took the captaincy away from him," Frankie said.

"Hassan's a really good player and I feel like if he left last season it would have been a big loss, but we have Ashleigh to fill his place, so we're still good," Oscar said.

Ashleigh's face grew warm at the compliment.

"Do you lot want to jog around the woodlands behind the clubhouse today for a change?" Frankie asked and the team agreed.

The woodland was a large area of land behind the clubhouse. It was densely packed with trees and home to many plants and animals. Towards the back of the woodland was a stream that provided a home for some woodland creatures, and a pond that local schools visited for pond dipping.

"This is such a beautiful area," Joanne said. "It would be such a shame for it to be made into flats."

It really would, Shay thought.

Joanne suddenly stopped. She closed her eyes with a smile on her face. "Listen to the sound of the birds. How beautiful is that?"

Everyone was quiet, even Jamie. The bird sounds were like a song, a procession of rippling whistles, gurgles, tweets, trills, screeches, and croaks. Something most of the children had never really bothered to listen to before.

"Nightingales, nightingales, nightingales," Jamie repeated before he continued his jog.

"Nightingales? What's he talking about?" Maxwell frowned.

As the under-tens looked at each other confused, the penny dropped for Shay and his eyes widened. "Hang on, I think Jamie's onto something! Mum, do you remember my summer topic for school on conservation? We searched up rare birds called nightingales and we listened to a recording of their singing on YouTube."

"Yes Shay, you're right," Joanne exclaimed. A smile spread across her face as she realised where Shay was going.

"Guys, if they are nightingales, that would be perfect to help us with our petition," Shay said as he tried to stop himself from jumping up and down.

"How can birds help us save our club?" Oscar frowned.

"Some birds are protected! That means you must protect their breeding habitat," Shay explained. "Like nightingales! They can't destroy the club or this area because it would ruin their homes."

"Jamie is a genius!" Oscar squealed.

"Yeah, nice one Jamie!" Frankie said, but Jamie was too busy doing cartwheels to pay attention.

Kathy smiled with pride at her son's knowledge and was glad he had given the other children a chance to see how smart he was. Jamie had a lot of interesting hobbies including belonging to a bird club.

"I know someone who's an expert on birds," Kathy said. "She's from Jamie's bird club. I'll give her a call and see if she can come down."

"Thanks Kathy, that would be great! Can you please tell her it's an emergency?" Shay pleaded.

Everyone put their hands together as if praying.

Kathy laughed. "I'll give her a call as soon as possible."

CHAPTER 26

The Darcheville Memorial Cup

It was a damp, chilly April morning when AC turned up at Marshals playing fields for the Darcheville Memorial Cup Under-Tens Tournament. Mr Darcheville had been a former player who had worked hard to support local players in the community before he recently passed away. The league and the local teams had decided to create a new tournament in his honour and named it after him.

The tournament had drawn a large crowd, including the local press and the local MP. Many clubs from around the area had signed up, so extra pitches had been marked out on the grass, covering the fields from one end to the other. It was packed with teams wearing every colour. There were volunteers wearing high-vis jackets, lots of portable loos and tents for first aid, drinks and food.

Rayne spotted the burger tent straight away. "Mum, can I get a burger and drink?"

"Rayne, we only just got here!" Joanne sighed.

Coach Joe waved the under-tens over, so Shay said bye to his family and went to join his team.

"Alright, first let me check if you're all here." Coach Joe scanned the team and looked at his watch, Oscar hadn't turned up yet. "I asked you to be here a little earlier today for a reason. Does anyone know why?"

The players looked around at each other and shrugged their shoulders.

"Is it because you like us so much?" Oscar asked. He appeared from behind Coach Joe and quickly sat down on the grass beside his friends.

The players laughed but Coach Joe wasn't amused.

"We need to have another word about your time keeping," he said sternly.

The smile fell from Oscar's face and for once he didn't give a smart reply.

Shay put his hand up. "Is it to do with Jamie's friend from the bird club?"

"No, but I think this will put a smile on your face." Coach Joe grinned. "I know you've all been worried about the sale."

The players looked around wondering what it could be until Frankie shouted, "Look!"

Their lion mascot, wearing the AC United football kit, appeared from the clubhouse. It began to dance and wave at everyone, jumping up and down excitedly. It caught the attention of the other teams who ran up to it.

"Coach Joe, who's inside the mascot?" Shay asked.

The players looked at him expectantly and Coach Joe said,

"Don't ask me, you're not meant to know,
You're just supposed to enjoy the show.
Copy its actions when it starts to prance
And let us see you do the football dance!"

The players laughed as they tried to copy the mascot's moves. It was the most fun Shay and Frankie had had in ages. Eventually, the mascot had to go, it waved and waddled over to the other side of the fields before it found a safe place to sit away from the little children who had been trying to grab hold of it to give overly enthusiastic hugs!

Coach Joe was right. It did bring a smile to their faces, and everyone felt pumped and ready for the match to begin.

"You've got three games to compete in," Coach Joe explained. "The top four teams will advance to the semis depending on how many points they have, then if we win the semis . . . we'll be in the final!"

"Come on AC, we've got this. Let's be the first team to ever win this cup!" Shay said.

The team cheered and high-fived each other.

"But make sure to focus on each game as they come," Coach Kaan said. "Each match is only ten minutes each way, which is why you must get straight in there from the get-go."

"Oscar, because of your lateness, you're going to have to sit out the first match and I will be speaking to your parents about this," Coach Joe said.

Oscar nodded as he hung his head.

After the warm-up, AC were ready for their first match against the North London Warriors. The grounds were packed with fans, officials and even football scouts. As there were so many matches playing at the same time, there were no commentators for the games except for the big final, to avoid any confusion.

AC United always wanted to play their best football, win games, and impress their coaches, but knowing actual football scouts were around felt beyond their wildest dreams. Shay knew that everyone would definitely be playing their best football, hoping to get spotted, and he was so glad that his ankle was better so he could play.

Shay glanced at Ashleigh, and he knew he would have to be a team player. He had to let go of any negative feelings he had towards her. If she was in a better position to score, Shay would make sure she had the ball. Today was about winning the cup as a team but he prayed that it would be *his* foot on the end of the winning goal.

CHAPTER 27

Nothing To Lose And Everything To Win!

All Cultures United vs The North London Warriors

The first match kicked off with an early foul from Troy, which led to The North London Warriors being awarded a free kick. Maxwell, the goalie, was on his toes with his hands stretched out to the sides. He hopped from foot to foot as the ball shot towards him and managed to block it with his left foot. With the ball still inside the box, Maxwell dived on top of it to keep it safe.

Jamie passed the ball to Shay who shot it at The North London Warriors' goal, but the ball ricocheted off the cross bar. Annoyed with himself for missing, but with no time to sulk, Shay played on.

The North London Warriors had a near miss when their striker slipped away from his marker and got a shot on goal, which had Shay screaming, "Mark up!" to the defenders.

Frankie ran the ball down the middle of the pitch and, at the last minute, crossed it to Jamie who managed to tip the ball into the goal past an unsuspecting keeper. AC were leading 1-0!

The AC coaches punched the air as the team ran over to a surprised Jamie and engulfed him in a massive hug. Shortly after, the final whistle was blown, without any further goals being conceded.

All Cultures United vs Alpha FC

After a fifteen-minute break including a snack of fruit and water, it was on to the next game. The second match was against Alpha. They were a local team, who would give AC a run for their money, and with Hassan missing down the centre it was good that Ashleigh could take his place. She was the perfect addition, with her speed and skill, and the players and coaches knew it. After a hard twenty minutes, with one foul against Jamie causing an Alpha player to be sent off, there were no goals either end.

The under-tens walked over to their coaches and noticed Coach Reece had arrived. Immediately the players felt excited.

"Alpha isn't an easy team to beat so not to worry," Coach Reece said. "This draw still gives us one point, so we're up four points now. If you win this one, we could be through to the semis!"

All Cultures United vs the Tottenham Rangers

"Tandeep, pass," Shay yelled, as he ran down the centre of the pitch with his hand in the air, signalling for the ball.

Running onto the ball, Shay saw Ashleigh inside the box. He hesitated for a moment, but Shay knew making the pass was the right thing to do. He passed the ball to her, and she left footed it straight into the back of the Tottenham Rangers' net! The AC fans went wild. Running over to Shay, Ashleigh high-fived him. Feeling that this could be a truce between them, Shay smiled as he ran back into the game.

"Great work AC, keep the pressure on!" Coach Joe shouted, as he ran along the edge of the pitch in front of the respect barriers.

Frankie intercepted the ball from the Tottenham Rangers' winger and ran full steam ahead with it. Frankie passed the ball to Ashleigh who took it down the left wing before crossing it over to Shay with pinpoint accuracy. Shay kicked the ball on the volley and giving the keeper no chance at all, the ball ruffled the back of the Rangers' net.

"Goooooal!" the AC fans screamed.

Shay was happy he had scored but he knew it was because Ashleigh had helped him.

"Great assist," Shay said to Ashleigh.

"Of course! We're both on the same side," Ashleigh replied.

And in that moment Shay realised that they did actually make a pretty good team. Now AC United were through to the semi-finals!

All Cultures United vs Finsbury Allstars

It was clear the semi-finals would be a tough game because AC were up against the Finsbury Allstars. Earlier in the season they had played a friendly against them, which had been a hard game and had resulted in a draw.

The Finsbury Allstars were wearing a red kit like AC United but because it was AC's home ground, the Allstars were asked to put a yellow high-vis over their tops to avoid any confusion.

The match got off to a good start as AC managed to control the ball in the Allstars' half of the pitch. Tandeep passed to Ashleigh, who passed to Jamie, who crossed it to Shay. But before Shay could kick the ball, he was pushed to the ground by one of the Allstars players. Shouts of "Foul" echoed from the crowd and AC were awarded a free kick.

The Allstars readied themselves in defence with their goalie bouncing on his toes. Shay decided the shot wasn't in range and he looked around at his team-mates. Tandeep's hand went up and Shay passed the ball to him before he ran forward. Just like they had practised in training, Tandeep quickly passed it back to Shay, who took the shot. The ball hit the crossbar. The keeper dived the wrong side leaving the goal open and Shay chased after the ball, to catch the rebound. He tapped it into the goal. AC were leading by 1-0!

Both teams fought hard for goals and there were many near misses. Finally, the ref blew the final whistle, and the AC players ran around the pitch in celebration. They had only scored one goal, but it was enough. They were in the finals!

Their celebration was short-lived when they realised who they were up against. It was their rivals The Highbury Bears. Last season Hassan had been injured by The Highbury Bears. AC had neither forgotten nor forgiven them for it.

CHAPTER 28

The Get Back!

All Cultures United vs The Highbury Bears

Everyone gathered to watch the final match of the day.

Coach Joe looked at his team with pride. "I don't care what the score is today, just continue to work hard, do your best and have fun. You've already done yourselves and all of us proud. You've made it to the finals! Hands in." Everyone piled their hands on top of each other. "3-2-1."

"United!" AC roared back.

Walking on to the pitch, both teams looked confident, but they all knew in their hearts there could only be one winner. The ref signalled for the captains to come over. Shay and Ted from The Highbury Bears eyed each other up. They shook hands, gripping each other tight.

"AC United starts the match today with Maxwell in goal, Blessing and Troy in the wide defensive positions, Ashleigh partners Tandeep in the attacking wide areas, with Frankie starting down the centre of midfield. Shay is the captain and striker!" Jay, the commentator roared, the excitement raised in his voice.

"And The Highbury Bears starting line-up is Zane in goal, Bertie and Jason in defence, with Casio and Jordan on the wings. Ted, the captain, in midfield and Lucas as striker," Jay announced.

The ref blew the whistle.

"The Highbury Bears midfielder passes the ball into the area, but Maxwell is alert to the danger and catches the ball with ease. He's kicked the ball high across the pitch," Jay said. "AC United's Ashleigh takes down the ball with great control and makes a forward pass to Frankie, who then passes it onto Tandeep."

Ashleigh's grandad was at the front of the crowd. He had his hands cupped around his mouth and shouted, "Nice play Ashleigh!"

Every parent was so excited that they began shouting instructions to the players with some even shouting at the ref!

Casio and Shay were one-on-one in a tackle. Suddenly, Jordan, The Highbury Bears right winger slid on the floor and tackled Shay, which caused him to fall forwards and land hard on his knees.

The ref blew the whistle and awarded AC a free kick. Shay stood up and brushed the dirt off his knees, and that's when he noticed he was bleeding. He wiped the blood away with his shorts, ready to get back into the game but Coach Joe called him over to have the First Aider check his knees. Although keen to get back onto the pitch to take the free kick he used the opportunity to catch his breath. Shay was surprised when Coach Joe signalled for Frankie to take the free kick.

Frankie adjusted the straps that held his glasses in place.

"Come on Frankie, you've got this," Shay shouted, walking back onto the pitch.

Frankie stepped forward while The Highbury Bears made their wall in front of the goal. When the ref placed the ball on the ground, Frankie steadied himself and took a deep breath.

I can do this.

He ran at the ball and aimed the shot over the wall, but the keeper made a fantastic save flicking the ball onto the bar. Disappointed, Frankie dropped his head onto his chest. He so badly wanted to score.

"Unlucky!" Jay boomed.

"Keep your head up Frankie!" his mum yelled from the crowd, as his team patted him on the back.

Disappointed, Frankie looked over into the crowd searching for his dad, needing to know that everything was okay. He found him and Colin gave him a thumbs-up.

"You've got this," he mouthed, which made Frankie feel a million times better.

AC continued to push hard with a few more shots at goal but Zane, The Highbury Bears keeper, arguably one of the best stoppers AC had played this season, was saving every attempt they made.

"The Highbury Bears have got possession and their striker is running through the midfield. Frankie is hot on his heels and using his pace to catch him up. Look at him go! Frankie's cut across The Highbury Bears striker and dispossess him of the ball. What a tackle!"

"Nice one Frankie!" Coach Reece shouted and Frankie grinned.

After winning the ball, Frankie turned away from the AC goal and made a run towards the opposition's goal, but the ref blew the whistle to signal the end of the first half.

During half-time the AC Mascot appeared and began entertaining the crowd, but at that point there was no time for AC to enjoy their mascot.

Coach Joe, Coach Kaan and Coach Reece called the players over.

"So far you've managed to hold them off but now it's time to step up your game," Coach Kaan said.

"I've heard they've got a couple of new players who I'm sure they'll be bringing on in the second half to change things up," Coach Joe said.

After a fifteen-minute break they were back on.

"There have been a few changes to both teams for the second half," Jay announced. "AC United have brought on Oscar, who has replaced Troy, while The Highbury Bears have replaced Bertie and Lucas with Omar and Hassan."

"Hassan?" AC yelled looking at each other and their coaches before looking across the pitch to see if it was *their* Hassan. It was. He'd been sitting on the bench the whole time with his hood up.

CHAPTER 29

Traitor!

"What a traitor!" Frankie angrily whispered to Shay.

"Now we know why he didn't want to talk about his new team," Shay responded.

They couldn't believe that Hassan had joined their rivals!

"Can you believe him?" Troy snarled.

The team glared at Hassan, who avoided their gaze. Instead, he took off his coat, to reveal The Highbury Bears kit underneath and high-fived his new teammates.

The second half was under way. Within minutes Tandeep crossed the ball to Shay, who took aim and drilled a beautiful shot from twelve yards, past the helpless Highbury Bears keeper, to make it 1-0.

"Goal!" Jay screamed, almost dropping the megaphone in his excitement. "And what a goal!"

The AC crowd went wild with shouts and cheers. Shay celebrated by jumping in the air, turning around, stretching out his arms and legs, while screaming "Suiiii!" in honour of his favourite player Cristiano Ronaldo.

Hassan put his hands on his hips and glared at Shay.

As soon as the ref blew the whistle to continue play, Lucas from The Highbury Bears kicked the ball into the path of Hassan.

"Just look at Hassan go!" Jay shouted.

Hassan steadied himself and kicked the ball that slipped underneath Maxwell's body and into the net.

"1-1!" Jay announced. "What a beauty of a goal by the former AC player!"

Hassan smirked at Shay and Frankie who grimaced back at him.

"AC is coming back strong and keeping the ball in The Highbury Bears' half but wait – Hassan has intercepted a cross from Tandeep to Shay and is now making a run down the centre towards the AC goal. Frankie is hot on his heels!"

Frankie caught up with Hassan and went straight in for a tackle. The two players tried to get their bodies between each other and the ball. Frankie managed to get in front of Hassan then pivot to the side, maintaining possession, he managed to do a back heel and pass the ball back to Shay.

"Not bad for someone who was on the development team last season!" Hassan shouted.

It seemed like every insult Hassan had thrown at Frankie was suddenly running through his brain, and before he could stop himself, Frankie pushed Hassan hard in the chest. Hassan stumbled and then a second later he threw himself to the ground holding his ankle. Right away, the ref blew the whistle and rushed over to him.

"He kicked me!" Hassan yelled, as he pointed at Frankie.

"No, I didn't!" Frankie argued.

But immediately the ref held up a red card and Frankie was sent off. Frankie pulled off his football shirt and threw it to the ground. He couldn't believe Hassan had got away with it! Hassan smirked as Frankie stomped off the pitch.

"That was a clear dive, everyone saw it!" Shay said to the ref.

Hassan stood up, hurt ankle clearly forgotten, as he walked away without a limp and fist-bumped his teammates.

The ref ignored Shay and blew the whistle, the game restarted. AC had to play on one man down.

The Highbury Bears made a dash for the goal but were blocked by Blessing and Jamie.

"Jamie has won the ball and skilfully feeds it to Tandeep. He makes a perfect pass into the path of Shay and look at him go! Now the AC captain is running through unchallenged and takes a shot. He buries his second goal to the left of the keeper to make it 2-1. GOAL!!" Jay screamed dropping his clipboard in his excitement. The list of all the players' names started to swirl in the wind and Jay had to stamp on the paper to stop it blowing away.

Everyone cheered for AC while The Highbury Bears looked on in silence, most of them with their heads down.

"Again, excellent work down AC's right, as Oscar and Jamie run down the flank, creating an opening. Jamie threads a through pass to Tandeep. Tandeep's got the ball and is running full speed ahead towards the goal. Hassan has run in to defend and is standing in his way but look, Tandeep's put the ball straight between his legs and retrieved it. He's nutmegged him! Tandeep's taken the shot and he's wrong-footed the keeper, the keeper's dived the wrong way and the ball's gone straight into the back of the net. GOAL!"

Tandeep slid along the grass on his knees, threw his arms into the air and surprised everyone by yelling, "COME ON!"

This was the first time Tandeep had spoken at football! AC rushed over to congratulate him for his goal and for finding his voice.

"It looks like every time AC United go forward they're creating chances at will. However, I must say, The Highbury Bears keeper is managing to keep the score line down with some epic saves," Jay continued. "AC United have forced a corner down The Highbury Bears right side!"

From Tandeep's resulting corner, which was swung in with pace, Shay flicked a left foot volley from the edge of the box, past the diving Highbury Bears keeper and into the goal. The team ran towards him and patted him on the back. Shay had now scored five goals in this tournament and AC were leading 4-1.

The final whistle blew, and the coaches and fans ran onto the pitch. Shay was hoisted up on his dad's shoulders where a big smile spread across his face. They had won! In the distance Shay noticed a tearful Hassan being consoled by his dad.

"AC United have won the first ever Darcheville Memorial Tournament and trophy!" Jay announced. "And the player of the match is Shay from AC United!"

Shay was so happy he could burst.

"Nice one Shay, you deserve it," Ashleigh said.

"Thank you, Ashleigh," Shay said, and he meant it.

AC climbed onto the podium to collect their medals. Shay stood in the centre ready to lift the trophy. Looking out at the crowd, their families and coaches, Shay couldn't believe that they had done it!

Frankie stood next to him smiling but the smile didn't quite reach his eyes. After being on a winning team how was he supposed to smile and be happy, then just leave and join a new team?

The competition organisers handed out gold-embellished medals with a green, circular centre and a gold and blue football in the middle. Written around the outline of the ball in white lettering were the words 'Darcheville Memorial Cup Winners' and the date.

Shay was handed the presentation cup trophy. It was a large golden bowl with presentation handles on the sides with traditional blue and white ribbons hanging from them. The bowl sat neatly on a gold stand with a heavy marble base. The plate also had the words

'Darcheville Memorial Cup Winners' and the date engraved on it. Shay lifted it up high above his head and immediately the crowd roared. It felt like the whole of North London were there cheering for them.

CHAPTER 30

The London Bird Club

Ever since the team had heard the birds singing, they had changed their daily mile route to the woodlands. Every time they went by the hawthorn bushes with their pretty white petals and pink anthers, the players slowed down and crept past in silence. They listened out for the birds they hoped would help them to save their club.

It had been a few weeks since Kathy had offered to speak to the lady at the bird club, and the team were keen to hear from her. Today, at the end of practice, the coaches introduced them to a tall, White lady named Donna. She had long, brown, straight hair and bright red lipstick. She was wearing a black raincoat and woolly hat and slung over her shoulder was a ruck-sack with bird pictures. Donna stood beside Kathy and Jamie, who was jumping from foot to foot.

"Hello everyone! Jamie and his mum Kathy told me about the possible sighting of nightingales in the Woodlands," Donna said. "Me and my friends from The London Bird Club, including Jamie and Kathy, have been over to the woodlands a few times to check it out and I'm pleased to tell you that nightingales are definitely inhabiting these woodlands."

Shay and Frankie looked at each other with eyes wide. Did this mean what they thought it did?

"I suggest you contact your local Councillor who should be interested in preserving this space," Donna continued.

"Are you saying that they can't sell our club?" Shay asked, wanting to make absolutely sure.

"They should really leave this area alone because the land they want to buy is home to these birds and is important for them to successfully breed. The birds are nesting, and their eggs cannot be disturbed," Donna explained.

"This is amazing!" Frankie said over the cheers from his teammates.

"Anyone know who the local Councillor is?" Shay asked.

"Yes, it's Councillor Shirley Crawford," Kathy said.

"I think we should give Donna, Kathy and Jamie a round of applause for all their help," Coach Joe said.

The team clapped for them, but Shay was so happy that he ran over and hugged Donna, Kathy and Jamie. Soon, the other team members joined in, and Kathy laughed as she was squeezed from all directions.

"Thank you," AC United chorused.

CHAPTER 31

The House

"Frankie love, you ready?" Tina called up to him.

Frankie sat on the edge of his bed and swung his feet. He pretended not to hear his mum. The last thing he wanted to do was to go and see another house. He wasn't interested in where it was or what it looked like. He wanted to live here, in *this* house that he had grown up in, on the same street as his best friend Shay. He wanted to play for AC United.

"Frankie, come on! Dad has strapped Sanchez into the car. We need to get going," Tina said.

Frankie sighed and slowly walked out of his bedroom. He sat in the backseat of the car without saying a word. They were tuned in to Radio North London, which announced the five o'clock news.

Colin noticed Frankie's sad face in the rear-view mirror. "You're going to like it Frankie, I promise you. You'll have your own room, a big garden, and a park around the corner to play football in."

What's the point if I can't play football with my friends? Frankie thought to himself. He pressed his head back into the seat and closed his eyes.

After driving for twenty minutes, the car slowed down and eventually stopped.

"We're at the new house," Tina said.

Frankie opened his eyes and looked out but all he could see were houses and trees. He didn't know where they were, but he realised that they hadn't gone very far.

Frankie looked from Colin's face to Tina's then back to Colin's before asking, "Are we still in North London?"

His parents watched him amused, before they both nodded and smiled. Slowly, the biggest grin crept across Frankie's face as he reached for his seat belt.

"Does that mean I can stay at AC and my school?" he asked.

"Yes, if we get the house," Tina said.

"Come on then! What are we waiting for? Let's have a look inside!" Frankie said, as he jumped out of the car.

The estate agent was waiting for them outside number twenty-seven London Road. The bricks had been painted in a cream colour and the three windows at the front were bare so they could see right inside. The downstairs room was empty, and the walls were freshly painted white.

As they walked towards the estate agent, she held out her hand and shook Frankie's parents' hands before opening the large, black front door with the glass panel. The house was clean and empty, and much bigger than their current house.

Frankie and Katie immediately went to explore. Frankie looked at the garden and decided it was definitely big enough to play football in. Then he went upstairs to choose a bedroom for himself.

"I'll have this one!" he called out. He stood in the biggest bedroom in the house.

"No chance! Over here Frankie, we think this one will suit you," Colin called back.

The bedroom was smaller and overlooked the garden, but Frankie thought it was perfect. He could already see himself living here with Shay coming round to play football in the garden and staying for a sleepover. The thought made him smile. He crossed his fingers for luck, hoping they would get this one.

*

"Aunty Tina and Frankie are at the door; shall I open it?" Shay asked as Joanne got up from the sofa to look through the window.

"I'll get it. You check over the letter for the councillor and see if we have included everything," Joanne suggested, as she walked towards the front door.

Shay heard Frankie's quick footsteps before he saw him. Frankie had a massive smile on his face.

"Shay, our new house is only twenty minutes from here! I won't have to leave AC or move schools if we get it!"

Shay threw his arms around Frankie's neck and the two friends hugged as they jumped up and down.

"Yesssss!" they yelled at the top of their lungs.

"Boys, keep it down!" Danny said as he came into the living room to join them. Shay and Frankie immediately stopped. "Shay, can you read out the letter we wrote to save the club? Let's see what Tina and Frankie think."

Shay grabbed the letter from the table and cleared his throat.

Dear Councillor Crawford,
Please don't let the council sell AC United Football Club. The London Bird Club has confirmed that nightingale birds live in the woodlands behind our clubhouse, and they are a protected species. That means the area

must not be disturbed. Our football club has been there for a long time and lots of children go there. We love it. If you sell it, where would all the players go? We don't want to go to any other club. Lots of people use the clubhouse for parties and the scouts use it on Tuesdays and Wednesdays. Schools use the woodlands for school visits and mini beast hunts, and our families use the grass for picnics and playing. We are starting a petition to save the club, but we need your help. Please help us.

Yours sincerely

The AC United under-tens

"That's a great letter Shay! Well done," Tina said.

"I'll type it out later and email it to the club to see if the other parents have anything to add before we send it to Councillor Crawford," Joanne said.

"Thanks Mum," Shay replied.

"You know what, I've got a mate who works at the local radio station," Danny said. "I'm sure he can help us spread the word. He might even let you come on to his show to talk about it yourselves. I'll give him a call tomorrow."

"Dad, that would be so cool!" Shay exclaimed.

"The radio reaches thousands of people," Frankie said. "I bet everyone will help us then."

CHAPTER 32

SOLD

Shay bounced impatiently on his parent's bed while Danny spoke on his mobile. Shay couldn't wait for his attention any longer.

"Dad, it's been over a week since we sent the email to Councillor Crawford. Why is she taking so long to get back to us?"

Danny held his hand up to Shay to wait a moment. A few minutes later Danny hung up the phone and said, "These things can take time but I'm sure we'll hear something soon. On the other hand, that was my mate Jerry from Radio North London. Remember I said I would speak to him about the club? It's a bit short notice but he would like you, Frankie, and your coaches to come into the station and talk about your petition tomorrow after the match."

"Tomorrow? That's sick Dad!" But Shay's excitement didn't last long. "Can you believe it's our last training session today? And our last game at Marshals tomorrow. I can't believe we could lose it all." Shay let out a long, sad sigh.

Danny walked over to him and held Shay's face in his hands. "You're amazing, you know that right? I'm so proud of what you're trying to do and *if* we lose Marshals, it won't be because of a lack of trying. Come on, let's get Frankie and see if we can organise the radio interview."

Shay tried to stay positive. They hadn't lost the club yet, so they still had a chance.

They pulled into the car park at Marshals and were met by a frantic Ashleigh who rushed towards them.

"Look at the clubhouse!" Ashleigh yelled, pointing towards the sign.

A large green and white poster had been stuck across the FOR SALE sign and on it in capital letters was the word SOLD.

"Dad, it's too late!" Shay cried.

"Hold on son, let's just wait and see what's going on," Danny said.

Danny, Shay, Frankie and Ashleigh rushed over to the pitch where the coaches were surrounded by the players and parents.

"Can I have your attention please?" Coach Joe said. He waited for everyone to fall silent before he continued. "As we can all see, our clubhouse and playing fields have been sold. The Council have asked us to refrain from using the clubhouse and pitch -"

Before Coach Joe could finish speaking, everyone began to talk at once.

"We can't use the pitch?" Frankie cried.

"How could they do this to us?" Shay asked.

"This is so unfair!" Ashleigh said.

Coach Joe sadly shook his head. "Our hands are tied. I know this wasn't the news we hoped for."

"Do you know if the council have exchanged contracts yet?" Jamie's mum, Kathy asked, and everyone looked at her. "Because if they haven't, then it might not be officially sold yet!"

"I'm not sure," Coach Joe admitted.

"Then we might still have a chance!" Shay said. "Me and Frankie have been invited to Radio North London to tell everyone about what's going on. They also want the coaches to come. Maybe someone will be listening who can help us."

"Well done boys, what a brilliant idea. We'll be there," Coach Reece said looking over at both Coach Joe and Coach Kaan.

"Definitely count me in!" Coach Joe said.

"Me too," added Coach Kaan rubbing his Nazar.

"We're going straight after the match tomorrow, so you all need to tune in," Shay said.

"I'll definitely be listening," Ashleigh said. Shay smiled at her.

"I'm sorry everyone but seeing as we can't use the pitch, we've had to cancel tomorrow's home game," Coach Kaan explained.

"Cancelled!" Frankie cried. Just when he thought everything was getting better it was now falling apart.

CHAPTER 33

Radio North London

On Saturday morning the club received an email from Councillor Crawford, which they forwarded on to the other families.

Dear AC United under-tens team,
    Thank you so much for your email. I was saddened to learn that your precious football club was under threat of closure. I would like to offer you my full support to try to save it. My suggestion would be to fight the proposal and sale on the grounds that the council's Biodiversity Plan states that, 'it must protect and enhance habitat for wildlife.' This means that the council should protect the space where protected birds

*like nightingales live and lay their eggs, I believe this
should do the trick.*

*Please let me know if I can be of any further help
and let me know how you are getting on.*

Yours sincerely,

Councillor Shirley Crawford

"Mum, what does bio ... that word even mean?"
Frankie asked Tina after reading the email.

"Biodiversity. It's a bit tricky to explain but it's to do
with looking after things that grow and live in your
area, wherever you live around the world."

"Like the nightingales in the woodlands?" Frankie
asked and Tina nodded.

"And it sounds like the councillor is on our side!"
Tina said. She opened her arms and Frankie ran into
them. "We'll win this love, don't worry."

"I hope so Mum," Frankie said.

*

The radio station was a small room with big computer
screens, a mixer, speakers, headphones and microphones.
Shay, Frankie and the coaches looked around the sound-
proofed room. Danny was sitting in the corridor until it
was over. They couldn't quite believe that any minute
now, they would be going live on air across North London.

"Welcome to Radio North London," Jerry said as he stood up in his seat. His bald head stopped just below the ceiling. "Before we begin, let me connect these microphones to your tops, then just say your name for the sound check."

Shay, Frankie and their coaches did as they were asked, and Jerry gave them all the thumbs-up. Shay and Frankie sat down in silence. Shay's heart was beating so loudly he was sure everyone could hear it. Frankie kept wiping his sweaty hands on his tracksuit bottoms.

"Boys, you look really tense, take a deep breath and relax. You'll be fine, okay?" Jerry said.

They took a deep breath and slowly they felt calmer.

A green light appeared on one of the screens, then the number five flashed up, followed by four . . . three . . . two . . . one.

"With me in the studio today we have Shay and Frankie from All Cultures United football club. And their coaches: Coach Joe, Coach Kaan and the original Baller Boy himself Coach Reece," Jerry said into the microphone. "Thank you all for joining me. Let's get straight into this and tell my listeners about why you're here today."

"We need everyone's help to save our football club," Frankie said. "It's not fair that the council want to sell the land to developers to build houses on."

"We don't want to see any bulldozers anywhere near our club," Shay explained.

"I see," Jerry said. "So, the Baller Boys are taking on the Bulldozers? Sounds like some real fighting talk. Can you tell the listeners what's so special about your club?"

"It's a place for everyone. Our friend Jamie comes to our club, and he's got ADHD. His mum says Jamie needs it because when he's there the coaches understand him, and he gets to be himself. Plus, he gets lots of physical activity and he loves football. He's so good at it," Shay said.

"Our club is called All Cultures United because everyone's welcome and we've got the best coaches," Frankie said. He looked over at their coaches who smiled at him.

"I heard that you made a surprise discovery near the club. Can you share it with the listeners?" Jerry asked Shay.

"Yes, we discovered a bird species called nightingales that live in the woodlands next to our club. Donna from The London Bird Club told us they're a protected species and should not be disturbed. Our local Councillor is supporting us, and she says we should appeal because of the bio, erm bio . . ." Shay stumbled over the word.

"The local council have a Biodiversity Plan, which promises to protect and enhance habitats for wildlife,"

Coach Reece explained. He winked at Shay. "And the nightingale is a protected bird. We plan to use it as part of our petition to keep the area as it is."

"Wow! I had no idea," Jerry said. 'So, Frankie, please tell us what we can do to help."

"We've started a petition, and this is what it says," Frankie said, reading it out loud. "All Cultures United Football Club and their friends are demanding that the local council re-think and stop the sale of Marshals playing fields, clubhouse and surrounding woodlands. This area is not only home to the AC United football team but also a protected species of bird called night-ingales. The players need a safe place to train and play football, and the nightingales need a safe habitat to live, which is what they both have now. We are calling on you to help us stop the sale. Please find our petition online and sign it. Oh, and everyone from our club also has a copy of the paper petition so people can sign that one if they'd prefer."

"That was brilliant Frankie," Jerry said. Shay gave Frankie a high-five.

"In three weeks today, we need everyone to meet up at our club at Marshals playing fields at five o'clock because we're going to march to City Hall and hand the petition to the mayor," Coach Joe said. "It's very important to get as many names involved as we can."

"Wow, thank you guys! I'm sure you've moved the listeners enough to take action and sign your petition. What I'll do is put the details on our website and across all our social media platforms to remind the listeners where to sign. I'd like to thank you all for coming in today, and I'm hopeful you will get the result you deserve. Good luck guys," Jerry said.

Frankie and Shay looked at each other with their fingers crossed. Now they would just have to wait and see if their interview would make any difference.

CHAPTER 34

The Demonstration

Today was the day. The march was announced in assembly and lots of students and teachers had promised Shay and Frankie they would show up to support them. The boys were hoping for a big turnout for the march to City Hall.

The morning had already gotten off to a good start when Tina received a call from the estate agents. She called Frankie over.

"Guess what?" she said.

"What?" Frankie asked, his heart beginning to race, as he hoped it wasn't more bad news.

"The house is ours!"

Frankie threw his arms around his mum. He was so happy he could cry. Now he would get to stay close to

Shay and as long as they could save their club, he could carry on at AC United!

After school, on the way to the march, Frankie told Shay the good news and Shay punched the air in celebration.

"That's wicked, Frankie. I'm so happy that you're not leaving," Shay said.

The feeling of this win gave the friends a new burst of energy and they felt more determined than ever to try to save their club.

They arrived to find Marshals playing fields packed! There were the coaches and all the players, the scouts, school children along with families and friends, The London Bird Club members all wearing black t-shirts with their logo, and people from the public who also wanted to save the clubhouse and land. Donna was holding a huge banner that read, 'Save AC United Football Club' and 'Save The Woodlands' which had been written in colourful capital letters. When she noticed Shay and Frankie looking over at her, she waved at them, and they waved back.

Many were holding placards up, with slogans such as, 'Hands Off Our Club,' and 'Baller Boys And Birds Need A Place To Thrive.'

"I can't believe it! Look at all these people." Shay gasped.

"Maybe they heard us on the radio?" Frankie said. "Come on, let's see if we can find the rest of our team."

The demonstration had been arranged to leave the playing fields at five-thirty. They were going to walk to City Hall to hand over the petition to the London Mayor. There were people wearing high-vis jackets, who were there to walk alongside the demonstrators, to help control the traffic and keep everyone safe. All the AC players were there, dressed in their football kit. They walked at the front of the demonstration with their coaches.

"Coach Reece, do you know how many people have signed the online petition?" Frankie asked.

"Well, the last time we checked it was thousands," he answered. "Hopefully it's enough."

The players looked at each other with wide eyes. Thousands of signatures! That was amazing!

Coach Kaan had put all the signed paper petitions in a trolley suitcase and was pulling it alongside him when Shay and Troy walked over to him.

"Coach, we'd like to pull them please as we want to hand them over to the mayor," Shay said.

"Of course, you can. There's stacks and stacks of paper containing over four thousand signatures from what we've collected, so it's heavy. If it gets too much for you just let me know, alright?"

"Thanks Coach but we've got this," Shay assured him.

Coach Kaan smiled and handed the trolley to Shay and Troy who pulled it together.

Rayne and Katie were standing with their parents just behind the team, they were carrying a banner that read, 'Children Need Places To Play,' which had been made by Joanne.

Ashleigh was holding a huge banner with Maxwell that had red writing that read, 'Ballers Not Bulldozers!' It had been painted across a large piece of white fabric that was taped between long sticks at each end.

The crowd set out walking through the streets chanting, "Save our club! Save our club!"

With his hands cupped around his mouth, a very animated Tandeep marched along yelling, "Save our club, save our club, 3-2-1 UNITED!" at the top of his voice.

The march took over two hours to reach City Hall and along the way there were photographers taking pictures and cars honked their horns in support.

The tall, glass, oval-shaped building came into sight. There were many people that couldn't manage the walk, like Shay's Grandma, who met them there. Shay's Grandma was wearing a red t-shirt that had 'SAVE AC UNITED FOOTBALL CLUB' written across the front in white.

The demonstrators marched straight to the front of the City Hall and stood at the bottom of the steps chanting, "SAVE OUR CLUB."

After a short while a door at the side of the building opened and a security guard appeared.

"Who has the petition?" he asked.

"We do!" the team shouted.

Shay lifted out the stack of signed sheets of paper and handed it over to the security guard.

"And there are more signatures online," Frankie said.

"Thank you. Someone from the office will be in touch," the security guard said then disappeared inside again.

"Okay . . . what now?" Maxwell asked to no one in particular.

Shay looked at Frankie who looked at Maxwell and shrugged his shoulders. None of them knew what would happen next. They just hoped they had done enough.

CHAPTER 35

An Unusual Season

It had been over a week since the demonstration and the players hadn't heard a single thing. The SOLD sign was still hanging on the clubhouse, and it seemed like all their efforts were for nothing. Shay and Frankie walked past the dreaded SOLD sign to enter the hall for the annual AC United presentation evening with their families. Many of the players would be awarded for both their team and individual achievements.

All the coaches, players and their families had been invited by the club to attend and celebrate another successful season at All Cultures United Football Club. It was usually a great event with lots of awards given out, food, drinks and a party, but this year there was an air of sadness. It was the end of All Cultures United as they knew it.

Shay looked around the room. It was strange to see everyone dressed up for the ceremony and not in football gear. He was even wearing a shirt and tie for the occasion that his grandma had bought him.

Coach Reece, Coach Joe and Coach Kaan were stood at the front of the hall with Pete, the club secretary. They were dressed in trousers, shirts, ties and smart shoes.

Shay smiled to himself admiring how well they had scrubbed up for the occasion. Coach Reece walked through the hall greeting everybody and Shay felt a flutter of hope. Coach Reece would be choosing this season's Baller Boys and Shay hoped he would be one of them.

The hall began to fill up and Shay noticed his grandma speaking to a group of people who were wearing t-shirts with ACLT written on the front in big red letters. From listening to his grandma and parents talk about ACLT, Shay knew it stood for the African Caribbean Leukaemia Trust.

Shay saw Ashleigh's family walk into the hall, but he hadn't noticed Ashleigh with them. Maxwell was sitting next to his dad, who always wore dark glasses to cover his eyes. Maxwell had once told them that his dad didn't see very well, and they knew that Maxwell helped him a lot.

"Look at all those trophies," Frankie said.

The trophy table was heaving with brightly coloured certificates, shiny cups, medals and trophies of all shapes and sizes. As the players eyed them up, they hoped for the same thing – to be given the accolade of Baller Boy by Coach Reece. A Baller Boy meant you were the best of the best: a player who is exceptional at football, passionate about the game, and can execute skills to perfection.

"I think you'll get one Frankie. You've done really well this season," Shay said as he eyed up the trophies . . . and he meant it.

"Thanks, and I think you'll get one as well," Frankie replied. He felt okay with the fact that Shay really was a very talented player.

"Good evening, everyone. Can you please take your seats?" Pete said.

Family members took a seat at one of the tables and the players went to sit on the benches at the front. There was a girl sat on the bench labelled under-tens, she had braids halfway down her back and was dressed in a jean skirt and colourful, flowery shirt. On her feet were a pair of stylish red and blue Jordans that looked familiar to Shay and the others.

As the boys scuttled along the bench towards where she was sitting, the young girl turned towards them and smiled.

"Ashleigh!" they said in unison.

"You look different," Shay said, taking in her skirt and floral top. He had never seen Ashleigh wearing anything other than her football kit.

"Why? Because I'm wearing a skirt?" Ashleigh asked amused.

"Yes, I mean no." Frankie blushed. "You look cool . . . just different."

Shay laughed as Frankie stumbled over his words. Frankie's ears turned red.

"On behalf of AC United Football Club, I'd like to thank you all for coming this evening. There's a lot to get through so let's get started. First, I'll hand you over to Coach Reece," Pete said as he led the applause, so everyone joined in.

"It's been a very difficult season for us but as usual

we have pulled together," Coach Reece said. He looked around the hall. "We know we have the most amazing players and families at AC and without you there would be no club."

The hall was still and silent.

"This season we have had our biggest battle yet, and each and every one of you did your bit to try and save All Cultures United and Marshals playing fields from being sold. This was spurred on by our magnificent under-tens team," Coach Reece said. "I think they deserve a massive round of applause."

Everyone nodded in agreement and stood up to applaud and cheer the team.

Frankie, Shay, and the team smiled at the applause, but in their hearts, they were devastated at losing their beloved club.

"Thank you all so much. Now on to the—" but before Coach Reece could continue, he was interrupted by the hall door opening.

Everyone turned around to see a tall, Black, slim lady with dark hair, in a blue jacket and skirt, walk down the centre of the hall. In one hand, she was holding a piece of paper in the air and in the other she held a worn black satchel.

The woman went straight over to where Coach Reece was standing and began to speak to him in a low voice. She then handed him the piece of paper.

"I'm sorry can you excuse us for a moment?" Coach Reece said to everyone.

Coach Reece signalled for Coach Joe and Coach Kaan to join him as he walked out of the hall.

"What's that about?" Frankie whispered.

"No clue," Shay said. He wished he could eavesdrop.

It seemed to take forever before the coaches and the lady walked back into the hall.

Coach Reece cleared his throat. "So, we have a bit of news. This is Councillor Shirley Crawford." At the mention of her name, people in the hall looked at each other in surprise.

Shay eyes widened. "It's her!"

"She has just come from a council planning committee meeting," Coach Reece said. "And she has something she would like to tell everyone."

CHAPTER 36

Surprises and Prizes

"Good evening, everyone. I'm so sorry for interrupting your awards ceremony but I thought you might want to hear what I have to say especially while you're all together," Councillor Crawford said. "The planning committee has reviewed the council's plans to sell your club and together with the protected birds plus the voice of the community, your petition has been declared a victory! The council have had no choice but to reconsider their decision and the sale has been stopped. AC United is no longer for sale!"

There was a moment of silence before the hall erupted with cheers. They had saved the club! Shay and Frankie jumped to their feet and hugged each other.

"WE DID IT!" Shay yelled throwing his arms into the air.

The whole team huddled together and shouted at the top of their voices, "We are the champions! AC United, forever!"

It took several attempts for the coaches to get everyone to sit down again. Councillor Crawford took a seat at one of the tables, shaking people's hands.

"Can I ask the under-tens team to come up to the front please?" Coach Joe asked.

The team stood up looking puzzled. From behind the trophy table Coach Reece pulled out a large piece of card and held it up for everyone in the hall to see. The team gasped when they realised what it was. The club had arranged for a huge cheque to be made out to the African Caribbean Leukaemia Trust (ACLT), the charity that helped Shay's Grandma when she was ill.

"Last season this amazing team arranged a sponsored run, which helped us buy a club mascot costume. They had some money left over and decided that they wanted to give it to a very special charity," Coach Reece said and everyone in the hall clapped.

Coach Reece gave the cheque to the team to hold while he asked the representatives from the charity to come up to the front. The two people that came to the front introduced themselves as Bev and Orin, they gave a short speech thanking the club and the team for their donation. "The African Caribbean Leukaemia Trust (ACLT) is a charity committed to providing hope to patients living with blood cancer," Orin said.

"We are very grateful for the donation and for your club's support and would like to thank all of these players," Bev said. She walked with Orin along the line of players shaking their hands.

Shay and Frankie handed them the oversized cheque and the clapping commenced again.

"Now, on to the main event, the awards presentations," Pete said. "The first award is for the most improved player of each team. For the under-tens, the award goes to Frankie!"

Frankie could not believe it. He looked at Shay who smiled so hard Frankie could see all his teeth. Colin clapped the loudest and was on his feet. Frankie walked to the front to receive his award in a daze. The gold trophy felt heavy in his hands.

Shay leaned over to Frankie when he sat back down and whispered, "I told you they'd notice you."

Staring at his trophy, Frankie felt so proud. He couldn't get the grin of his face as he read the words Most Improved Player over and over again to himself.

As the award's continued, Maxwell was presented with the Manager's Player of the Season Award. The Player's Player Award went to a surprised Ashleigh. This award was voted by the team and AC United had accepted Ashleigh as one of their one. With her trophy in her hand, she high-fived the boys on her way back to her seat.

The Top Scorer Award was next, and as Coach Joe lifted the golden football boot sounds of 'Ooooh' and 'Wow' could be heard throughout the hall.

"And this award, which is truly deserved, belongs to a player that we all need to keep an eye out for in the future. Congratulations to Shay," Coach Joe announced.

Shay jumped to his feet with a huge smile plastered across his face. It felt amazing that all his hard work had been recognised.

It was time for the final award of the evening and except for Jamie, who was sitting on the end of the row tapping his feet, shaking his legs and whistling, the under-tens sat in silence with their fingers crossed, frozen in anticipation.

"Here at AC, we are always on the lookout for exceptional players and this season there have been a few across all the teams. It has been AC United's pleasure to coach and teach potential stars."

Coach Reece held up the Baller Boy trophy, which sparkled in the light. It was a round, white, frosted-glass football on a red stand, with Baller Boy engraved on it and the player's name written in gold on the plaque at the bottom. The trophy was truly special, and the players stared at it longingly.

After the speech, Pete called out the names of the Baller Boy winners from all the teams, while Coaches Reece and Joe handed out the awards and shook the players' hands. Finally, it was time to hear who would be crowned Baller Boy from the under-tens team.

Shay closed his eyes and whispered a prayer. He had a feeling it was between him and Ashleigh and he desperately hoped to hear his name.

"The under-tens Baller Boy Award for this season, is presented to someone whose commitment never waivers, who is exceptionally skilful, a natural leader and a great team player," Coach Reece said. "Congratulations Shay!"

"YES!" He jumped out of his seat holding onto his Top Scorer Award and skipped over to collect his Baller Boy trophy. While standing at the front he looked towards his family and friends who were on their feet cheering for him, and the loudest cheer of all was from his grandma.

At the end of the presentations, the parents swarmed to the front of the hall to congratulate and take pictures of their children and thank the coaches for a great season. A photographer took individual pictures of each team, then she took a club photo with all the teams and coaches together. The photographer placed Ashleigh right in the middle of the group next to Shay.

Ashleigh leaned over and whispered to Shay, "One day I will be one of Coach Reece's Baller Boys!"

"Oh, me too!" Frankie joined in, overhearing Ashleigh. "Shay better enjoy it while it lasts." But he grinned at Shay to show he was being playful.

Shay looked at Ashleigh. It may not have been the smoothest journey but Ashleigh being part of the team had pushed him to work harder. In fact, the entire team was stronger because of her, and they all knew it. Shay turned to Frankie with his heart bursting with happiness that he was staying at AC.

Shay laughed. "May the best player win!"

Acknowledgements

Thank you to Raia-Sunshine and Shay for listening and listening, your patience was admirable.

Special thanks to football mum Saranna Maynard for encouraging me to kickstart this book and to Adella Charles for her critique of the story.

To Shugar Dean, big thanks for helping me find the right words to explain the tactical moves when my brain got fuzzy.

A huge thank you to Donna Zimmer from The London Bird Club for her advice and suggestions on protected birds and for making me aware of the biodiversity plan to protect habitats.

To Lyndsay, my friendly librarian, thanks for the company and cups of tea while I sat in the children's section of my local library to write.

Thank you to my wonderful publishers and editors Abiola and Helen for believing in Baller Boys.

Finally, a huge shout out to Kerry Janes who was there from the start and for all the last-minute late nights that got me over the finish line.